Robert Bourne

Safe Sex is essential: your very life may depend on it. Please remember that some of the sexual practices that are featured in this work of fiction (written in an era that pre-dates lethal STDs) are dangerous and they are not recommended or in any way endorsed by the publishers; by the same token, we do not condone any form of non-consensual sex for any reason: it is reprehensible and illegal and should never become a part of a person's real life: rather it should remain firmly in the realm of sexual fantasy.

ORGY GIRL

Past Venus Press
London 2006

Past Venus Press

is an imprint of

THE *Erotic* Print Society
EPS, 1st Floor, 17 Harwood Road,
LONDON SW6 4QP

Tel: +44 (0) 207 736 5800
Email: eros@eroticprints.org
Web: www.eroticprints.org

© 2006 MacHo Ltd, London UK

ISBN : 1-904989-26-8

Printed and bound in Spain by BookPrint S.L., Barcelona

No part of this publication may be reproduced by any means without the express written permission of the Publishers. The moral right of the author of the text and the artists has been asserted.

While every effort has been made by PVP to contact copyright holders it may not have been possible to get in touch with certain publishers or authors of former editions of some of the titles published in this series.

ORGY GIRL

Robert Bourne

*E*PS

Chapter 1

There was no avoiding Karen Shaw once she walked into a room. The statuesque brunette stood a fraction under six foot in her bare feet, and her long, jet-black hair fell straight past her waist, brushing the tops of her buttocks. That long, straight hair made her look even taller than she was, and to this she sometimes even added boots or platform shoes with four-inch heels. Yes, she stood out in a crowd, but not just because of her height. Her tall frame was covered with the juiciest arrangement of flesh any man could hope for. Her tip-tilted breasts were large and firm and, despite their size, didn't need a bra to hold them up, her waist was slim; her belly and hips were full-fleshed and somehow very, very suggestive.

Today she wore a halter-top that let the bottom of her breasts swing free, and exposed her midriff to the bright sunshine. She also wore a pair of faded dungaree shorts that started about four inches below her cute navel. They ended just an inch or two below her crotch – a crotch that had driven men to do dangerous and foolish things. Her legs were golden tan from the sun. She was sitting in a swing made from some rope and an old, worn-out tire. She swung back and forth from the branch of an ancient, gnarled oak, swinging her legs so that her bare toes brushed the top of the neatly manicured grass.

"Hey Mike," she called gaily. "Mike, come here and swing me. I haven't done this since I was seven."

Mike, tall and bronzed, rose from his deckchair and walked around behind her.

"I'd rather swing with you than swing you," he said, placing his hands on her full, rounded ass and pushing forward, sending her soaring up towards the outstretched, leafy branches of the giant oak.

Karen swung back to Mike, and again he pushed her forward and upward, making sure to get a generous handful of her ass. They were alone today at Mike Huxted's Long Island estate that he had inherited from his parents. He usually spent all summer here at the mansion in East Hampton and always invited friends to stay for a couple of days or weeks, whatever. The estate rolled over ten acres and had it's own dock for sail and powerboats.

Karen swung back and forth, feeling the wind against her face lifting her long hair, sending if flying in all directions. The wind also lifted the edges of Karen's halter and Mike could see a flash of breast, a hint of cherry-red nipple as the wind toyed with the edges of Karen's lacy frock. Back and forth, higher and higher Karen swung with Mike pushing her. At the top of each swing she kicked her long legs up high, almost touching the leaves of the tree with her big toe, making no attempt to keep her top from billowing out and baring her breasts to the winds and the skies.

With each trip of the swing Mike got more and more turned on. He was grabbing a handful of her ass each time she passed him and he wanted more. On her next swing by him Mike reached out and quickly undid one of the snaps at the back of Karen's halter. She squealed as he did it, but again she kicked up her legs as she approached the branches of the giant oak, letting her now partly loose halter swing free. Mike waited patiently for Karen to make the return swing, and this time he managed to free another of the three snaps. Karen squealed again, laughing as she made the upswing and kicking her legs up again.

This time the halter flew up in Karen's face, entirely baring her breasts. Mike watched with his mouth open as Karen's breasts rolled back and forth, their rich, red nipples becoming sharp and pointed. She pushed the halter back down but it didn't do any good because as she swung by Mike he undid the last of the snaps and the halter fell away, floating in the air current created by Karen's swinging and falling to the ground.

Slowly, Karen slowed her swinging down. Her breasts juddering back and forth as she swung through the warm summer air felt good. She looked around for Mike but couldn't see him. Still on the swing she undid the snaps of her dungaree shorts and squirmed out of them tossing them in the air and letting them float off. The smooth rubber tire felt good against her bare ass as she continued swinging and looking for Mike.

She swung back and forth, her head thrown back looking up at the leaves above, letting her hair fly wildly in the breeze when she suddenly felt Mike's hands grab her and pull her from her comfortable seat. She fell to the ground and wrestled with him, trying to break free from his grip. She felt him flip her over, and for the first time she looked at him and saw that he had shed his clothes.

"So you went and hid behind the tree," she said, laughing, then breaking from his grip and running across the lawn.

Without a word, he pursued her and again caught her and pulled her to the ground. They rolled over and over in the soft grass, her long, smooth, muscular legs tangling with his. She wrapped her legs around him firmly and locked them together, trapping him. Mike struggled vainly, but he couldn't break loose.

Karen was strong. He continued to squirm and eventually managed to turn himself around until he was facing her. Somehow his mouth was now right at the bush of black hair behind which her sweet, juice-laden slit was hidden.

Mike grinned. He lashed out with his tongue, poking through the hair and running his wet, pink tongue up and down her soft, wrinkled cunt-lips. He felt a shudder run through her body and he felt the grip of her legs around his waist loosen, but this time he didn't try to break free. He continued lapping his tongue up and down in long leisurely strokes. From bottom to top and from top to bottom, very slowly, keeping an even tempo.

Karen lay back, completely relaxed now, supporting herself on her elbows. Her head rocked from left to right as she fell deeper and deeper under the spell of Mike's slow, rhythmic lapping at her cunt. Her long hair swept back and forth, brushing through the grass. Her legs had locked themselves first but were now spread wide open to receive Mike's tantalizing, teasing tongue. Her buttocks alternately squeezed tight and then relaxed, pulsating to the rhythm of Mike's licking. Her labia were suffused, swollen and firm. Their colour was a dark, angry pink.

Karen felt the pressure beginning to build, and now she slid forward, trying to get Mike's tongue into her twat deeper, but Mike pulled back, keeping his tongue only at the doorway to her pleasure hole. Now Karen started moving up and down in the direction opposite to the one Mike was working in. As she got more and more excited, her body began to shudder. She brought her thin, long-fingered hands to her large breasts and squeezed them gently. They were full, firm and ripe and her cool fingers felt good against the warm flesh. Her nipples were hard, and their points were tender to the touch. Slowly she dragged her hands across the sensitive skin, one finger at a time, lingering a little each time one of her fingernails touched her aching nipples.

Her breath became more and more shallow as Mike speeded up the movements of his tongue. She groaned softly as she felt herself relinquish control of her body and felt the orgasm welling up and taking over her consciousness.

"Now, Mike, now!" she whispered, summoning up all her strength to utter those three words.

Her prayers were answered as Mike suddenly shot his tongue out and stuck it deep into her honey pot, licking up the sweet, fragrant juices that now exuded from her swollen cunt flesh. He felt her body buck and toss as she came again and again while he made circular motions inside of her, wrapping his tongue around her clit, and pulling on it; poking his tongue deep into her slit and running it up and down the back wall of her vaginal tunnel. She pressed her crotch against his face urgently, as if her cunt were some great, cavernous maw and she was trying to swallow up his entire head.

"Take me, Mike, take me," she cooed, "please – just fuck me!" She felt the first waves of orgasm from the cunnilingus fading away. She sank down until she was flat on her back and then she spread her legs in blatant invitation.

Mike advanced further up her body on all fours. His penis was hard, bouncing and quivering with lust and eager to do its work. He crawled forward slowly, the mauve glans shiny with clear pre-cum juice, his long, thick shaft gliding like a torpedo towards its target. Their faces were even now, and he leaned down to kiss Karen. She took his mouth and poked her tongue into it, still tasting the remnants of her juices. She loved the taste of herself mixed with his sweet saliva, and she ran her tongue around his this way and that, licking the last vestiges of her pussy juice that remained in his mouth.

She felt his hands on her big tits; grabbing them firmly and squeezing them, bringing her relaxed nipples back to stiff erection. Her legs were spread apart as far as she could stretch them, so far that her cunt-lips had poked through the dense swatch guarding them. The edges of her pussy-lips were pink and glistening with the juices of her first orgasm. She could feel the tip of his prick bouncing low enough to just tap at her cunt-lips, she wrapped her arms around him and tried to pull him up into her, to swallow his delicious tool.

She squirmed under him, rubbing her breasts against his hairy chest and feeling his prick swing back and forth just touching and tantalizing her anxious cunt. Slowly he lowered himself onto her, letting his cock head part the thick labia of wet her twat a little at a time, rationing out the pleasure, so that she didn't come too soon. Then the head of his prick sank fully into her cuntal passage – she sighed – then a little bit of the shaft – she groaned – then he let a little more sink in – she whimpered, and finally he shoved it all the way in until it kissed her cervix.

"Aaarrgh," she cried, bucking and convulsing under him.

And now he started in earnest, pushing and pulling, tugging and shoving, in and out, over and over again, with smooth, powerful strokes. He felt the waves of pleasure wash over his body. Karen was moving with him, grinding their hips together, feeling his chest slam against her breasts. Again and again, he didn't let up. Karen's mouth fell wide open, but she was paralyzed and couldn't scream the scream of pleasure that she so wanted to let out.

Suddenly she felt him tense. Mike was about to come, and the very thought sent her reeling into some sort of sensory stratosphere where, paradoxically, she was feeling so much emotionally that she could feel almost nothing physically. Intuitively, Mike slowed down. In fact, he wasn't ready to come yet, but he guessed that Karen couldn't last much longer, and he was right: her body circuits overloaded and she tried to scream but only a gurgle emerged from her throat as the orgasm hit her hard. Her body became stiff as a board; she lost control of herself and lay gasping and twitching spastically below Mike while he continued to plunge his cock in and out of her, not giving her a moment's rest and getting her body churning again.

But for a moment Karen's body did relax. It was like the momentary calm before a storm. Her toes unclenched and she eased her grip on Mike's back. The hot, pink flush that had spread across her chest retreated slightly, but only for a moment as she felt the passion stirring in her again under Mike's continued thrusting. Her breathing became shallow once more and now her body ached for more and more as Mike's cock continued to penetrate her in the most delightful way imaginable. She cried softly as she felt him continue, she craved the moment when the juices that were stored up in his tight balls would spurt freely into her expectant, clamouring womb. She hungered to feel the source of life which was within Mike's body rush furiously into hers, she needed more than those earlier signs of his impending climax, she wanted the real thing, pints, quarts gallons, oceans, of Mike's cum to pour into her and inundate her so that her loins were awash with their combined sex juices.

"*Owwaarrgh,*" Mike groaned as his body went stiff. He could hardly move, he had lost control of the finely toned machine that was his body and now all the tensions that had built up would rush madly out of his body and fill Karen's to overflowing. Karen knew what was going to happen next and she laughed and started to shift her legs into the optimal position. However, before she could move them more than an inch, Mike's entire body convulsed and his back arched. She sensed, rather than felt, his semen roar into her gully like a flash flood, while his pubis ground down onto her clitoris provoking a gasp of pure pleasure from her. Mike shot his abundant sperm over and over again into her very, very wet cunt. Soon the thick fleece of her pubic bush became sticky and matted as their juices were forced out of her tight vagina by his last desultory thrusts, oozing over her

swollen cuntlips, trickling down over her anus and beyond, down even into the crack of her ass cheeks.

Slowly, very slowly, Mike started to recover from his orgasm. His cock began to shrink and came out of her with a little 'plop'. It released a further flow of juice. He rolled off Karen and lay close beside her, smiling as he watched her reach into her cunt and scoop up the white, gooey semen that continued to flow out of her temporarily stretched vagina. She licked her fingers, which she had poked into her pussy. She offered them to Mike who tasted his own stuff mixed with hers. It was sweet and sticky, he thought and there was plenty of it. He liked it.

Karen laughed.

"You know, should bottle it and sell it. Really."

They lay in the shade of the tree.

"I've had offers," Mike said with a smile, watching as Karen now put both her hands to her twat to catch the juices that were dripping out. Both her hands were coated and she put them to her breasts, smearing them with her sticky hands in a large circular motion. Her breasts glistened as she spread the liquid over them, and then poked into her crack for another handful of the lovely goo that Mike had squirted into her. Slowly and methodically she continued painting her body until her big, firm breasts gleamed in the dappled sunlight, smiling at Mike as he rested and watched her.

She threw back her head, brushing all of her hair behind her and then lay down on Mike, her glistening sticky body, clinging to his, as they dozed off in the shade of the giant oak.

As Mike dozed he saw images of the days gone by flash through his mind, and the day, in particular, that he'd first met Karen Shaw.

He'd heard a lot about her, but had never met her. Mike Huxted spent a lot of time on the party circuit, and had attended more than just a few orgies. All of his money had been inherited, so he didn't have to do much by the way of work – just keep an eye on the lawyers and accountants. And at every orgy he'd heard the same thing over and over again, "you haven't been to an orgy until you've been to one with Karen Shaw."

He'd gotten intrigued by this build-up and started looking forward to the day he finally ran into her. A couple of months ago he'd been invited to an orgy and his hosts, Kimberly and Ronald Witt, had told him that Karen Shaw would be there. And that was all the invitation he needed.

"Do you know anything about her?" Mike asked Kimberly.

"Only from the few brief talks we've had. I know she's been to college and that she worked as a secretary for a while, and then as a dancer, but when I asked for more details, she would just change the subject. She's just a little mysterious – nobody seems to know much more about her, really. But what does it matter. You'll have a bang-up time if you can nail her," Kimberly laughed. "But remember," she warned, "I want you first."

"Sure," Mike replied, glad to take care of Kimberly if he could only have a shot at the intriguing Karen Shaw.

The Witts certainly knew how to throw an orgy. They had their own four-story townhouse in the East 70's and there were plenty of softly-furnished alcoves and hidden corners where guests could adjourn to once they found someone of their liking. Of course, the kitchen was well stocked with food and booze and there was always grass, hash and coke to be had. Unlike many other hosts, the Witts never rushed anyone to leave, guests were allowed to stay overnight or even for a few days if they behaved nicely, and there was plenty of room and plenty of loving.

The rich couple usually invited a dozen or so people – four or five men and seven or eight women, so there was always enough to go around. When Huxted showed up at the door, Kimberly answered it, and the gorgeous redhead practically dragged him in before he could even smile a hello, and before he could even shed his jacket she was in his arms, whispering, "Kiss me, you fool."

Mike gave her a hug and a long, deep kiss, tasting, not unpleasantly, the booze and smoke on her. It was obvious from the slightly unfocussed look of her eyes that Kimberly had been drinking and smoking for a while before he'd arrived. He surveyed the room and saw that he didn't know any of the people there except for Ron Witt, Kimberly's thickset but athletic husband. Ron would never win a male beauty prize, but nonetheless radiated an aura of power that was very sexy to most of the women he knew. Ron waved to him and then turned his attention to the two women he was with, both short: one was plump with a well-rounded figure, and the other thin, with full, prominent breasts. In a corner there was a willowy blonde wearing a see-through blouse with nothing under it and a pair of hot pants that revealed a saucy curl or two of her thatch poking around the edges of her outfit.

The blonde had a drink in her hand, and had her other hand firmly planted at the point where the legs of her hotpants came together. She looked warm and content and Mike smiled at her, as he felt Kimberly's hand grab his and pull him off into a corner.

"Your mystery girl, Karen Shaw isn't here yet, sweetheart, so let's go upstairs. I've got a

Orgy Girl ★ 19

surprise for you," Kimberly whispered.

She led the way and Mike followed, to the room adjoining the master bedroom.

"This is our surprise: only Ron and I know about it," she said as she pulled a drape to reveal a one-way mirror that provided a full view of the master bedroom.

Mike looked down at Kimberly. She and Ron were both in their 40's, but Kimberly could do more to him than a 24-year old. She was five foot four inches and had a perfect figure, with breasts that still had the firmness of a teenager's, a tiny waist and full, lush hips that housed the prettiest pussy in Manhattan.

Before she'd met Ron, Kimberly had been the highest priced call girl in town, and anyone who'd had her said she gave the best blowjob in the world. Of course, Kimberly was retired, and it was only Ron and a few close friends who got to enjoy her skills now.

Kimberly stood in front of Mike watching Ron and his two friends getting ready to swing into action. Mike looked at Kimberly and felt his cock rising filling the scant space in the crotch of his tight jeans. Tonight she wore only a sheer tank-top and a handkerchief-sized micro-skirt that revealed the bottoms of her well rounded buttocks. They both watched as Ron stripped and flexed his muscles, while the two women slipped out of their clothing, very seductively wiggling and squirming across the room.

They could see Ron getting turned on, as the two girls did a seductive little dance across the room, letting their breasts swing free. They pushed Ron down on the bed and climbed on top of him, the plump playmate squatting over Ron's face and teasing his mouth with her pussy, snatching it away and pushing his head down, each time he tried to stretch up for a bite or lick.

The slim dish meanwhile was busying herself by tantalizing Ron's tool, running her tongue up and down and poking the tip of her tongue into the little hole atop Ron's weapon.

Suddenly the curtains snapped shut. For a moment Mike was startled. The room was dark and he could hardly see anything. He had been very engrossed in the scene being played out on the other side of the mirror and had made a mental note that he'd have to have a shot at the slim creature who was eating Ron.

"Enough looking, lover boy. Let's have some action," Kimberly breathed is she stepped out of her tiny skirt. She had already pulled off her tank-top and now stood stark naked before Mike. She rotated her hips slightly, beckoning to him with the thick bush of red hair that grew between her legs and seemed to him like a flaming beacon for her cunt.

Mike quickly took the hint and undressed while Kimberly went to the bed and arranged herself, turning first this way and then that, letting her ivory skin rub against the black satin sheets. She pulled Mike down to her and gave him a long kiss, pushing her tongue deep into his mouth and letting it curl around his own. His cock hardened immediately, and he tried to push Kimberly down on the bed, but she fought him, staying on top of him and kissing his entire body, working her way down from his mouth to his chest.

"I'm gonna suck you dry, you big mother-fucker," she breathed as she took his cock into her mouth and started tonguing its shaft. Suddenly Mike felt very hot, he felt his cock twitch and he felt that he was about to lose control. He gritted his teeth and tried to regain his composure, but he couldn't. Kimberly was still the best blow job in town and now she was bent on extracting his semen against his will.

Kimberly stopped sucking his cock and looked up at him.

"I'm thirsty, you mother-fucker. Don't fight me, I can make you come any time I want," she said, laughing throatily. Then she dived back down and took his cock in her mouth.

She switched tactics. She stopped sucking and now started biting gently all along his hot shaft, and then abruptly she sucked again, and this time she took the entire length of him down into her throat. Mike couldn't hold out against this virtuoso performance. Once more, he felt Kimberly open her mouth even wider than before and swallow his entire shaft, her lips brushing his pubic bush just as it spurted the first jet of its sweet jism down the gorge of her throat. She gurgled happily as she felt his juice sloshing in her mouth and spilling down her gullet. God, he tasted good, she thought to herself.

Quickly she backed off and clamped her fingers around the base of his cock, shutting off the flow. Under her, Mike lay in an agony of curtailed pleasure, wondering what Kimberly held in store for him. He found out very quickly.

Still keeping her fingers clamped around his dick, Kimberly scampered around and put the head of his cock against the small opening of her ass. Mike felt the head of his prick penetrate the opening slightly, and then Kimberly released his cock, letting it spurt the rest of its load into her eager ass, letting it lubricate the tiny hole so that his massive prick would slide smoothly into her tight little asshole. She sat on him and rode him up and down, up and down, as she'd seen movie cowboys do, only instead of a horse, she had a stud, a super stud, under her, and his big dick was firm and strong and it penetrated her ass so deep that she could almost feel his cock poking into her stomach.

The faster she rode him, the more she could feel the pressure building inside of her until she could stand it no more. Suddenly, without warning, she went almost catatonic – all of the energy in her body slipped away and she surrendered to her orgasm, shaking and shuddering, her mouth wide open in a silent scream.

Lying under her, Mike could almost feet her tight little sphincter twisting his cock off as it clenched and unclenched spasmodically, forcing him to prolong his orgasm and continue to squirt his come deep into Kimberly's ass. She slipped off of him as his cock shrank back to normal, and lay beside him, his arm around her panting.

"I can still give a hell of a ride, can't I, lover boy?" she asked between gasps.

"If you were still making me pay for it, you could still charge the highest rate, hot-pants," Mike complimented her as he, too, took a few moments to regain his breath.

As they lay there, the door opened and Mike caught a glimpse of the lissome bombshell who had been eating Ron earlier. Following closely behind her was a tall, sensationally beautiful girl and it didn't take Mike a minute to figure out that this was the

Karen Shaw he had been waiting for.

"Oh, I didn't realize someone was in here," the shorter woman exclaimed.

"That's all right, honey," Kimberly spoke up. "I was just leaving. Karen, I want you to meet Mike Huxted. Mike, Karen."

Mike was staring at Karen fixedly. She was wearing a micro frock that barely covered her hips, and made her long, long legs look even longer.

"Hi," Mike said.

"Hello," Karen replied, coolly.

"Mike, this is Ruth Manetti," she said, distracting Mike for a moment. He turned and smiled at her, but was still unabashedly gazing intently at Karen.

"Ruth, why don't you come with me, sweetheart, and let these two become acquainted? I'm sure you'd like a drink," Kimberly hinted, getting out of bed and taking Ruth by the hand, and leading her to the door. The blonde woman looked disappointed, but followed obediently.

"You two kids have fun now," Kimberly laughed as she towed Ruth out of the room.

The door closed with a loud click. Wordlessly, Karen turned and walked to the door and threw the bolt, locking the room. She stood for a moment in the shadow of the door. Mike noticed that three of the buttons on her frock were already opened, and now he saw Karen reach for the fourth button and pop that one open, too. Then the fifth button – and the six – and the seventh. Somehow, this was the most exciting striptease he had ever been privileged to witness. Perhaps it was the utter lack of inhibition, the total self-assuredness, the almost animal litheness of this small act that got to him. But later, much later, he worked out what he had found so exciting about that brief moment. It was that Karen was in control. Karen was dictating the terms of their encounter. She was writing the script as she went along and poor Mike was like a mere bit-player in the presence of a star performer.

Mike wondered at her large firm breasts and the expanse of tanned, olive skin that stretched from between those breasts down to her navel. Very slowly and deliberately, taking another step forward, she popped the eighth button open, and then the last.

Almost as if she were bored, Karen stretched her arms out and pulled the frock open, sliding her hands out of the armholes and shrugging off the frock so that it slid down her long and slender legs to the floor. She stood before him now, a beautiful, seemingly endless expanse of olive skin, except for her dark, cherry-red nipples that seemed to be perched at the very points of her rounded, sloped, up-tilting breasts. Only one thing remained hidden and that was the pleasure spot, still behind a pair of flowered bikini-panties that really hid very little. She put both her hands to her waist and moved them down, spreading the bikini's waistband and sliding it over her hips and letting it slip to the floor. His eyes were glued to the thick thatch of dark pubic hair that sat at the base of her belly. Her right arm snaked out and hit the light switch returning the room to the semi-darkness in which Mike had just fucked Kimberly.

"Ready for more?" Karen asked Mike, who was still reclining in the bed taking in the sight of the amazing specimen of womanhood who had just stripped.

"Whenever you are, my love," he answered, shifting to give Karen room to lie down.

"Jesus," she said, "I'm horny as hell, don't play with me, just fuck me to death."

Mike could feel her hand reaching out and encircling his cock. The performance Karen had made out of undressing had made him erect again, and he was ready, willing and able to scramble her brains with his cock. It was as if he and Kimberly hadn't done a thing.

"Fuck me, lover boy, fuck me," she said, her voice as low and as sexy as Mike had ever heard. Mike rolled over and covered her body with his. She had stretched her legs in a graceful split, almost like a ballerina, and her gash protruded from her crotch. Her cunt lips were wide open, and Mike could see a thin film of shining pussy juice along the pink ridge of her cunt lips. She tugged on his cock and pulled it to her, inserting its tip into her and pulling Mike down on top of her so his prick slid all the way home to the back of her gash.

Despite her size, Karen had a nice, snug cunt, Mike discovered. It was deep, certainly, but warm and tight. She wrapped her arms around him to hold him still while she moved under him, so despite the fact that he was on top of her, it was she who was fucking him. Up and down, up and down, she tossed and moved doing all the work. Mike marvelled at the strength in her, and at the smooth, yet tantalizingly textured cunt walls that were sending shivers of pleasure racing through his body.

"Let loose, come on man, squirt into me," she gasped, still tossing Mike up and down. "I'm coming, I'm ..."

Mike felt her body convulse, and then felt his own bodily tensions go over the crest and he could feel himself shooting his spunk into her. He could also feel the walls of her cunt contracting and wringing every last drop of his semen out of his cock. He'd never felt anything like it.

The rest of the evening was lost in a blur. He was hot for Karen, and although he made it with two or three other women, it was Karen he really wanted. He pursued her all night long and at last she promised to come out to his estate for a visit.

When he woke up, Mike could see that Karen had been awake for a while. As a matter of fact she had been sucking his cock for a while, too, while he was still off in slumberland. His dick was only partially hard, but when he was fully awake, it stiffened to its full glory very quickly.

Karen climbed over his legs and straddled them revealing the hungry lips of her cunt.

"My daddy was in the Army and he always said, "If it moves, fuck it!" Karen laughed as she neatly tucked his dong into her and started moving up and down, feeling his swollen hardness stimulating the walls of her slit.

"Your daddy was a very wise man," Mike said as he watched the young Amazon fuck the daylights out of him.

It didn't take long before both of them came again, their juices intermingling in Karen's hot, tight cunt. And then, again, they collapsed like balloons from which the air had been released.

Karen got up.

"I'm gonna shower and head back for the city," she said to Mike.

"But you said you'd stay for a couple of

weeks," he complained, "and you've only been here for one."

"I know, but I gotta get back to work," she smiled.

"You never told me what you do," Mike countered, still mystified by this beautiful woman who seemed to have no visible means of support.

"Oh, I do a little of this and a little of that," she smiled.

"Why the big secret?" Mike asked.

"Nothing," she grinned as they walked back to the house. "I kinda wander here and there and get some bread together, that's all."

"Come on, what do you really do?"

"Nothing, really, lover boy," she said, smiling.

"I'm an orgiast... and you can look that up in your dictionary."

Chapter 2

Mike kept trying to get the truth out of Karen, but she just laughed and put him off as they showered and dressed. As Karen was getting ready to leave, he tried to get amorous again, but as willing as Karen was for a fucking as good as Mike could give her, she dodged this attempt. She had another appointment to keep, and she didn't want to be too tired when she got there.

Mike kept on at her, and finally let her go when she promised to come back next month. Meanwhile she slipped behind the wheel of her little scarlet MG and settled in for the drive back to the city. Tonight, Karen thought, was going to be the big night. Tonight's orgy was going to establish her reputation. Everyone who was anyone would be there, and tonight they'd all discover Karen Shaw, the greatest of them all.

The long drive into Manhattan was uneventful and Karen let her mind wander as her car rolled over the miles of concrete that led back to the city and her big assignment – the biggest of her career. She thought back to her first introduction to sex. That too had been at an orgy, though she was too young and naive to fully understand an orgy or what it was, but she soon caught on. Yes, those were the days, when sex was still a mystery, before she had decided to become an orgiast. But that first experience had really turned her on. She was in her senior year in high school, just seventeen years old, and still a little gangly and awkward, but her beauty was beginning to reveal itself. She had already grown almost to her full height, the result of which was twofold; first, she was taller than most of the boys so she didn't have many dates, and second, she was star of the basketball team.

Most of the girls were just discovering sex, and in the locker room after games there was always a bit of good-natured teasing as the girls compared their still-swelling breasts, or the scrubby growths of hair that were beginning to grow between their legs. Several of the girls had experienced sex, but Karen hadn't – not until the end of the first semester when her Coach, Linda Tree, asked her to stay after practice. Karen didn't quite know what to expect, especially when the Coach added, "and don't get dressed after your shower."

Karen went into the shower with the rest of the girls and washed herself and dried herself as they did, but instead of getting dressed like them, Karen wrapped a towel around herself and walked into the Coach's office.

"Hey, relax Karen, honey," Linda started, "I'm not going to ball you out or anything, so don't worry! I just wanted to check you out and make sure that you were all right – a physical, in other words. Why don't you take off your towel and sit down in that lounge chair?"

Karen smiled, relieved that everything was okay and that the Coach wasn't upset at her playing. She'd heard of physical examinations, indeed had been on the receiving end from doctors or nurses, but never from a basketball coach. Even so, she didn't think much of it, and besides, she was comfortable with her body and had few inhibitions about stripping off.

Linda Tree had been a professional gymnast and her body, which was superbly fashioned, was very well muscled, every one of those muscles hidden by the curves of he super-feminine body. She wore her short, honey-blonde hair in a stubby ponytail. She looked every bit the professional sports instructor: she was sitting at her desk, and after putting Karen at her ease and offering her a seat, she stood up, and watched for a moment as her young pupil let the towel drop from her body, still damp from the shower.

Linda was wearing a grey sweatshirt over navy shorts and now, to Karen's astonishment, she pulled the sweatshirt over her head and flexed her arms back, pushing her firm, muscled breasts forward. Karen watched her Coach avidly because she had never seen her in the nude before. Linda stooped slightly and pushed the shorts down her firm, well-shaped legs and let them slip all the way down. Karen stared at the triangle of golden hair that bushed around Linda's crotch. Her Coach was a beautiful woman, and Karen hoped to be that beautiful, too, someday. But now she just felt uncomfortable. She felt a twitching, a nervousness. Her eyes were riveted at her Coach's slit. The hair around it was the same golden colour as the hair on her head, and through the silky fringe, Karen could see pink labia that framed a darker slit, not unlike her own.

"Don't be uncomfortable honey," Linda said, correctly assessing her emotions. "We're both adults – women – and we don't have to hide our bodies from each other. I've seen you in the nude while you showered so its only fair that you should see me too, isn't it?

Karen nodded at the dubious logic of this as Linda walked around the desk toward her.

"You're a very pretty girl, you know that?" Linda asked.

"Thanks, Coach," Karen said, trying her best to relax and return the bright smile Linda had given her.

"Why don't you call me Linda," the Coach started. "I'd really like us to be friends. Now the reason I invited you here was so that I could examine you and make sure you were all right, so why don't you lean back in the chair and let it tilt back so I can have a look at you, okay sweetheart?"

Karen leaned back and the lounge chair reclined all the way. She looked up, blushing, and saw Linda smiling at her, but she still felt very uncomfortable and, at the same time, a strange sort of pressure was building up in her, one that was both physical and emotional at the same time, one that she had never experienced before. Linda separated her legs, and before Karen knew what was happening, she felt the Coach's fingers pushing through the covering of hair that had, for some time, begun to grow more thickly between her legs.

Suddenly the feeling of tension eased, she wasn't sure why, but later, when she tried to analyse it, she knew that the 'pressure' that had built up inside her was, in fact, pure sexual tension. When Linda's hand touched her pussy, suddenly the whole problem of sexual morality had been removed from her – she was no longer the one making decisions. Karen felt warm all over, and felt her body growing hotter and hotter despite the fact that the locker room was usually quite chilly. She also felt Linda's hand poke through the hair and reach for the swelling lips of her pussy and spread them apart ever so gently. Karen felt her hips moving upward almost involuntarily toward her Coach's hand. Linda's hand moved higher up the slit, until she reached the bud-like clitoris, and then, very carefully, she pinched it between her fingers and twisted it very gently, right to left, left to right and around and around.

Karen didn't know quite what was happening, but she knew that she liked it. She also knew that she had trouble breathing as she once more felt the pressure build and build within her body – subtly different to the kind she had just experienced. Once more it was like nothing she had ever known before. She twisted and turned, rubbing her bare skin against the rich leather of the lounge chair, tossing like a bronco, but being very careful not to get away from the hand of her Coach.

Rockets started going off in her head and she felt her pussy suddenly get very wet as if she had peed involuntarily and a giant heat wave pass over her and then disappear completely, leaving her lying spent on the chair, a thin film of sweat covering her entire body and a strange, wet, sticky juice covering her pussy hair and her thighs.

"Well, Karen, I think you'd better have another shower and then get dressed, and I'll see you at practice tomorrow," Linda said.

"Sure, Coach, I mean Linda," Karen smiled still a little shaky.

She pulled herself up and as she rose, Linda offered her a hand to help her and then embraced her in a long hug. Karen briefly returned the hug in an uncertain sort of way and then quickly made her way back to the showers.

By the time she finished showering and dressing the light was out in Linda's office, but as she was leaving she heard a sound in the Coach's office. She peered through the darkness and could see Linda lying on the lounge chair just as Karen herself had. Linda had both of her hands buried deep in her golden triangle. Her body was moving unevenly. Karen was fascinated. She stayed to stare as long as she dared, hardly breathing in case the sexy Coach detected her presence.

Several times more Linda asked Karen to stay, and several times she asked other girls on the team to stay. Karen wasn't quite sure what it all meant, and she was afraid to ask. One day, just before the Christmas break one of the other girls who she knew had also 'been asked to stay' approached Karen just as they were leaving the locker room after practice. Her name was Nancy and she knew Karen only slightly. The one thing Karen knew about her for sure was that she wasn't a virgin and that she masturbated a lot, at least that's what she always talked about in the locker room.

Once Nancy proved that she wasn't a virgin by lying down on a bench and pulling her legs wide apart so that everyone could see that she had lost her virginity.

"Hey Karen," Nancy began. "Linda and her husband are having a little party at their place Saturday night, wanna come?"

"What kind of party?" Karen asked.

"Oh, just a little one, just you and me and Slim Hendry, you know, the black guy who left school last year, and Linda and Don, her

Orgy Girl ★ 37

husband," Nancy replied.

"What's going to happen?" asked Linda with a certain amount of apprehension.

"Come along and find out, baby," Nancy said teasingly, "you'll really enjoy it." She put her hand around Karen's ass and squeezed it slightly and winked.

"Sure, why not?" Karen said slowly, thinking about the hint Nancy had dropped. Yes, why not, she thought to herself.

"Good, I'll pick you up at eight," Nancy said as she headed for her next class.

Karen wasn't sure what to wear to the "party" so she wore a simple semi-dressy frock. She was glad when Nancy arrived to pick her up and was wearing something similar. Karen tried to draw Nancy out about what would happen, but Nancy remained mum. She had heard about Slim Hendry, the black star of last year's football team, but didn't know much about him. She heard the same kind of rumours that everyone else had heard, that he had gotten a couple of girls pregnant and that he had slept with many more, that the size of his… but before she could reflect on the "party" any more, they arrived at the apartment house where Don and Linda Tree lived.

A tall, handsome man, someone who looked like a former athlete, opened the door.

"Hi darling," he said breezily to Nancy,

"and whom have you brought for us tonight?"

"This is Karen Shaw. Karen, meet Don Tree."

"Oh yes, Linda told me all about you Karen, come in, let me take your coats," he said. "Your outfits are ready in the guest room."

Karen followed Nancy not knowing what to expect. As they walked into the guest room, Nancy held up two tiny robes.

"Which one would you like?" Nancy asked Karen, "and will you unzip me?"

Karen pulled Nancy's zipper down, and selected the red and yellow robe. Nancy didn't say anything more to her, but simply continued undressing, shedding her bra, panties and stockings. Karen had seen Nancy in the nude before, when they had both dressed and undressed in the locker room, but somehow Nancy's body looked quite different in the dim light of the small guest bedroom. She was much shorter than Karen and had a well-formed body with generous round breasts. Her stomach was flat and hard and the triangle of hair between her legs was a dark, rich chestnut colour.

Karen started undressing too, watching Nancy as Nancy donned the blue robe that barely covered her snatch. Karen slipped the other robe over her body, couldn't help comparing her own body to Nancy's. Karen was much taller than Nancy and her breasts were higher and firmer, but Nancy's were larger. Nancy's legs were a little on the plump side, but Karen's were longer and more shapely. Karen's pussy was still visible through its light covering of hair that had started to grow around it, and Nancy already had a thick curly snatch. Karen let her mind wander for a moment to how it would feel to run her fingers through Nancy's little 'garden' and briefly pulled her finger through her own triangle, but then quickly took her hand away and straightened the tiny robe on her body so that it just about covered her slit.

"C'mon honey, let's meet the gang," Nancy said leading the way back to the living room.

Karen followed along to the living room when they found Don looking through the bedroom door watching Linda and Slim on the bed.

"Slim's been here for a couple of hours and Linda was kind of horny, so I told them to go ahead," Don said by way of explanation. "We've got something special planned for you later, Karen honey, so why don't you make yourself comfortable while Nancy and I loosen up a bit."

Karen's eyes were on stalks. Nancy giggled and Karen could see that Don had already gotten a hand under her robe and was running his hand around her ass. Nancy and Don headed back to the guest room leaving Karen at the door. Karen turned her gaze towards Linda and Slim. She was still stunned at the sight of the two of them on the bed, Slim was so black and Linda was so white that their bodies contrasted sharply. Linda was on her knees bending over Slim who was lying flat on his back, squirming slightly, but with a huge grin on his face. Linda had her face in his crotch and Karen couldn't see his cock because Linda had somehow managed to swallow all of it. Now she was letting it out of her mouth a little at a time.

When it was all out of her mouth, she squatted over his massive tool and lowered herself onto it, riding up and down gently, letting it ream her cunt thoroughly. Karen had never seen anything like it before and she watched fascinated not even aware that her own body was getting hot and that she was breaking out in a sweat despite the fact that she was wearing practically nothing. Linda rode up and down on the massive shaft that she was sitting on, and Slim arched his back so that his tool would be forced deeper into Linda. As Linda came down and Slim pushed up, their hips came together in a soft slap, a slap that quickly became rhythmic, like the beat of a metronome. Again and again, her pale white skin crashed softly into his shiny black skin and there was a soft slap, slap, slap.

Linda started groaning softly at first and then louder as she continued riding the stud beneath her, and the soft steady slap, slap, slap of their bodies merging continued until Linda could take it no more and suddenly, quickly, it was all over. Karen listened and watched as she heard Linda's strangled cry and saw her shudder, frozen in mid-motion as she came. She could also see that Slim had come and that some of his juices were overflowing and dripping out of Linda's cunt, and dribbling down the inside of her legs.

The two rolled over and disentangled their bodies and rested for a moment. Karen, still perched in the doorway, had never had sex before but now she wanted it, craved it and felt she couldn't wait another moment for it. Her virgin cunt was aching for a shaft to split it open and teach her about the pleasures of life.

Linda motioned for Karen to come into the room, so she stepped through the doorway, letting her robe fall open as she approached the bed with the two spent lovers, panting and regaining their breath. She slipped the robe over her shoulders and let it glide to the floor as she advance to the foot of the bed, standing naked before them, silently offering them her body. Slim's beautiful, ebony body glistened with sweat as he lay smiling up at her.

Wordlessly, Linda motioned for Slim to leave the room and when he did, she offered his spot to Karen who had remained standing, looking down at her Coach and her handsome black lover. Karen got on the bed on her hands and knees, advancing catlike toward where Linda lay. She hovered above Linda, her long hair brushing Linda's cheeks. Karen let her hair swing back and forth, and then lowered herself to kiss Linda, letting her tongue shoot into the Coach's mouth to duel with her tongue. Linda was getting aroused again, and though Karen didn't know what to do, she let her instincts take over. Karen brought her chest down on top of Linda's and let their breasts brush each other. She could almost feel sparks as their nipples came in contact.

Karen could feel Linda's hand probing her abdomen and then past her belly button; Linda smiled at the thought of this aggressive young virgin, and quickly poked her fingers into her sparsely-haired cunt and twirled her fingers through the slender strands, working her way in to the slit and fingering the innocent, but burgeoning, clitoris. She propped herself up on one elbow and then rolled over, pushing Karen down on the bed and lying on top of her. Karen was much taller than Linda and she could wrap herself entirely around her teacher as Linda lay on her. Linda's body, still sweaty, slipped easily over Karen's, as the teacher crawled down the length of her eager pupil until her mouth was at her virginal pussy.

"Oh, fuck me, eat me," Karen cried as her body became more and more demanding. "Now, now – "

Linda was ready, willing and able to oblige. She pulled Karen's cunt lips apart and, with her teeth, sought out her clit and started nibbling it very gently, getting it used to her teeth, but Karen still wasn't satisfied, even though Linda's busy fingers were sluicing up and down her virginal and very wet pussy-lips.

"Eat me, oh fuck, oh shit, yeahhhh... please bite it... fucking bite it off," she screeched between gasps, her little profanities sounding daring, but appropriate somehow.

Karen's body was bucking and twisting wildly now, and Linda had trouble hanging on to the clit with her teeth, so she clamped down harder as the juices flowed from Karen's cunt, wetting Linda's face. And then Karen couldn't take it any more, her body gyrated wildly, just once and then went rigid as she felt herself come, fireworks exploding inside her head, spectacular rocket-bursts making flashes of coloured light.

The two women were equals now, thought Karen. Before Linda had been the teacher and she the student, but although Karen still hadn't been penetrated, now she had had a genuine orgasm and that, at least, placed her on the same level as Linda.

After a brief rest, Linda took Karen by the hand and led her to the other room. Along the way she picked up a bottle that looked like it contained perfume. Linda led the way into the guest room, where Slim, Don and Nancy were fucking on one of the guest room's twin beds. Karen's mouth fell open when she saw the activity of that threesome. Nancy was supported between Slim and Don as they stood thrusting hard into her, leaving her legs dangling in the air. Don had his cock in her cunt and Slim had shoved his into her asshole. Nancy's breath came in short gasps as both men moved in and out with a smooth, synchronised piston-like movement. Karen had only heard smutty locker room talk about anal sex – much of it coming from Nancy herself. But somehow she couldn't imagine what it would be like to be fucked in the ass. Now she could actually see a lively demonstration.

Linda motioned for Karen to lie down on the second, unoccupied bed. Karen obeyed but she couldn't take her eyes off the threesome. God, she hoped that they would do that to her. She thought about the two immense cocks that were at this moment drilling into Nancy, oh how she wanted them! Oh how she wanted them both inside her at the same time!

Linda spilled some of the liquid in the

bottle into her hand and started massaging it into the sweaty pores of Karen's body. Karen was practically unaware of what Linda was doing to her, her eyes were riveted on little Nancy pinned between the two huge men who were showing her no mercy. Nancy bucked and screamed as she started coming in a massive orgasm that started somewhere in the general area of her ass, then spread to her lovely, pink, dribbling gash. She was experiencing the unheard of double pleasure and she was still pinned and couldn't move.

Both men eased off now to let her enjoy her orgasm. First Slim sat down, with Nancy still impaled on his buggering pole, and then Don gently disengaged, allowing her to fall back into Slim's arms, who held her while shudders of pleasure ran through her body, her asshole twitching spasmodically around his enormous black cock.

Now Don turned his attention to Karen. She could see his erect penis, still shining with Nancy's juices, waggle obscenely as he crouched over her. Then he lay down beside her and ran his hands slowly over her oiled body. Before now a man had never touched her this way and a shudder of intense excitement raced through her body.

"Do it, do it now, Don," whispered the impatient virgin, "just fuck me, fuck me hard!"

"Hey... just be patient, little one," Don

smiled.

But Karen couldn't wait. She spread her legs and pulled Don down on top of her, taking his tool in her hand and guiding it into her slit. It went in a little at first and then a little more. There was a brief hiatus and an almost unbearable pressure that suddenly gave. She felt her hymen being ripped open in a sharp flash of pain. But the pain was nothing compared to the pleasure of having lost her virginity. She pushed her hips higher to take in more of Don. The Coach's husband, who was being driven wild by this crazy young virgin, was only too glad to oblige. He brought all his weight down and rammed his shaft into her cunt, pushing deep against her womb.

Karen gasped just once and then was overcome with the sensations racing through her body. She ground her hips under Don making his tool wiggle and squirm inside of her. Don pulled his hips back and started making the slow rhythmic in and out movements. Karen's body was supercharged. She started moving her hips up to meet his and she heard the soft slap, slap, slap, that she had heard earlier when she watched Slim and Linda humping.

It felt good, oh, it was the best feeling ever, his cock ramming into her, their hips slapping together. Damn! It felt so good that she was going to... And then Karen came, like a volcano. Her cunt muscles contracted gripping Don's cock like a vice. She could feel the muscles of Don's athletic frame tense up and then he, too, was coming hard, making one last, deep thrust before lying very still on top of her. She could feel his cock twitch slightly and then open up and pour into her, filling her tight, virginal slit with thick male sperm for the very first time. He thrust a few more times, and the friction of his hard tool was much less. He started to shrink inside her and then his cock slipped out of her, followed by a little rush of blood-tainted cum.

"Jeez, honey, did you really come just then?" asked Don, his face registering utter amazement. In his not inconsiderable experience, seventeen-year-old virgins simply did not orgasm when they were deflowered.

"Oh yes, Don, thank you, you wonderful man. And I came so beautifully, too. With Linda, as well. Thank you both!"

Karen lay back, and for the first time since Don had started banging her she was able to look around and see what the others were doing. Slim still had his awesome machine in Nancy's ass, but Nancy was on all fours now and Linda was under her with her tongue vigorously working over Nancy's big, protuberant clit, and while they were still humping that way, Karen curled up in Don's arms and fell asleep, a proud and contented smile on her lips.

* * *

Karen snapped out of her reverie as she guided her car through the tunnel back to the city. Her first sexual experience had really been a superb affair. She remembered that after that brief sleep, Nancy had fingerfucked her, and later, she had been allowed to eat Nancy and Linda, so for the first time she was able to experience what her own sweet cunt tasted like.

Before that evening was through Karen had been fucked by Slim, doggie fashion, while Don used her mouth. Then they swapped ends. They both ejaculated within seconds of each other, Karen savouring the tangy sperm that Slim's outsized black cock spewed between her lips. After Slim and Don had worked her over, Nancy and Linda had taken over. Karen seemed to recall coming a dozen times that night. Not bad for a virgin, but she was sore as hell for a week after that little party.

Her memories of that initiation had affected her, and as she pulled up in front of her destination, Karen discovered that she was sitting in a puddle of her own pussy juice that had pooled on the leather seat of the MG. Well, she thought, within the very next hour that anxious little cunt of mine is going to have more than it can handle. And, she added as an afterthought, my future should be secure.

Meanwhile, she pulled a spare pair of sheer bikini panties out of her bulky purse and smoothed them down. She hiked her micro-skirt up around her waist and slipped the wet pair down over her hips, to the floor and let them drape over the accelerator pedal. Karen pulled a handful of paper tissues from her purse and wiped herself dry. She also wiped the seat and then poured two drops of Dior into the palm of her hand and massaged it thoroughly into her crotch, stopping only when she found that she was starting to excite herself.

She pulled the fresh panties on quickly, smoothed her skirt and stepped from the car.

Well, Karen thought, it's now or never. And drawing a deep breath, she walked up the steps to the door of the well-kept brownstone and rang the bell.

Chapter 3

It took a few moments for the door to open and Karen could hear the sounds of the party. The music was loud, with a funky beat to it, but did not quite succeed in drowning out the sounds of sex – the panting, the squealing and the grunting. A handsome young stud answered the door wearing a pair of scant briefs that barely contained his engorged cock.

"Hey there. You must be Karen," he said as he lounged in the doorway and looked her up and down, with a cool, supercilious smile that she found quite attractive. His cock hardened as he watched her and Karen could not help but notice it. She swayed gently. Let her hips jut out ever so slightly. Two could play it cool, she thought. I'm going to fuck him before the evening's out, though. Then I'll show him what cool is...

"And you must be Paul," she smiled back, hitching her skirt up a little to let even more of her thighs show.

With a show of reluctance, it seemed, he stepped aside just far enough to let her enter. Karen squeezed through the doorway, allowing her firm buttocks to press fleetingly against Paul's cock. It felt good against her ass, and if Paul was getting turned on, then – she had to admit – so was she.

Paul pointed her in the direction of Jeffrey and Diane Lester, the hosts of this little affair. They all shook hands rather formally, but the ice was quickly broken when the golden-haired hostess pulled Karen towards her and gave her a deep, lingering kiss on her mouth. Karen felt the older woman's wet, lithe tongue slip quickly between her lips until it touched her own. As she led Karen upstairs, Diane explained that their son had just turned sixteen and this party was being given in his honour. Today he would learn about sex from every woman here, and if sixteen-year-old Pete was excited about that prospect, so was practically every woman in the house, because for the past couple of summers little Pete Lester had had them all creaming in their pants as he wandered around the country club swimming pool.

Karen followed Jeffrey and Diane up to their room. If she could make a good impression on them, then her reputation as a super-orgiast would be assured and she'd be much in demand all around town. She looked Jeffrey over: he was tall with hair as black as her own and a mat of thick hair almost entirely covering his body. Christ – the guy was good-looking, but he was as hairy as a fucking gorilla! Fortunately, Karen liked a hairy man as much as a smooth one. Variety, she always thought, was the spice of life. Diane was a slender strawberry blonde – almost fragile looking, with clear, delicate features that could have been made out of Meissen china – and with small perky breasts; Karen could see them through the almost transparent shortie gown she was wearing.

"You wanna know something, hon? You really turn me on," Diane said to Karen, taking Karen's hand and leading her to the bed. "I'll bet that you have a nice, soft, wet pussy for me and Jeffrey to suck on, don't you?"

Karen smiled, and without taking her skirt off, let her bikini panties slip from between her legs to the floor. They were showing traces of moisture, and Jeffrey scooped them from the floor and sniffed them.

"Sweet as honey," he said with a lecherous grin as he continued staring at Karen.

Karen was used to the stares and decided to make the most of them. She led Jeffrey and Diane to the bed and pushed them down and then stepped back. An idea occurred to her. The music was just as loud here as it was downstairs. Something was playing with a deep, earthy beat that started to get to her. She was going to do her little dance, and she was going to do it like she'd never done it before. She gyrated her hips around in a circle and then made a similar motion with her shoulders. The movement of the shoulders sent her big breasts jiggling and rubbing against the sheer fabric of her blouse. Her nipples grew fully erect and strained against the blouse as Karen started twisting and turning her body slowly at first, and then speeding up the tempo. Her hair flew in every direction as she gyrated madly, her breasts danced as if they had a life of their own, straining against the fabric of the blouse, springing free through the low-cut neckline, and then bouncing back under the flimsy blouse.

Karen's body was coated with thin sheen of sweat as she speeded up her gyrations. Her cunt lips were rubbing furiously against each other and she was getting excited. Her dancing had caused her skirt to ride high up her thighs and as she continued Jeffrey and Diane could catch flashes of the dense black bush that shielded her twat. Diane was holding her left breast in one hand as Jeffrey fondled the other, her other hand was between her legs furiously fingering her aching clit. Suddenly Karen slowed down and planted her feet wide apart and started doing the limbo dance, bending back as far as she could and wiggling under an imaginary bar. She felt the cool, air conditioned breeze as she spread her legs and squirmed toward her hosts. Her cunt lips parted behind her black bush and suddenly she felt herself pushed backward into the deep pile carpet. Diane had leaped from the bed and had plastered her open mouth against Karen's cunt and was hungrily lapping up the sweet juices that were oozing from that honeypot.

Karen lay back catching her breath after her lively dance, her face entirely, sexily, covered by her long, black lustrous hair.

A pair of small hands parted her thighs, and Karen felt cool fingers trace a line down her closed labia, gently opening them up like the petals of a flower to reveal the sopping wet interior of her cunt. The fingers were quickly replaced by Diane's long, inquisitive tongue...

The dance itself had excited her enough, but now she felt Diane's tongue making slow, even strokes, vainly attempting to lick her cunt dry and lingering lovingly over her clitoral bud that Diane had exposed by pulling its hood back and up. Her tongue point explored every nook of Karen's labial folds, sluicing up and down between the inner and outer pussylips, even stabbing the little pucker of her asshole from time to time. Karen's breathing became steady and then rhythmic as she felt her body wind inexorably towards a massive orgasm like some giant clockwork spring. Karen's hostess had a very educated tongue and she enjoyed a good cunt almost as much as she enjoyed a good cock.

Diane was on her knees; bent over Karen's crotch, with her own ass perched high in the air as she sucked Karen avidly. Jeffrey had had more than any man could take watching his pretty wife sucking one of the most beautiful cunts in the world, with her own cute cunt and asshole on proud display. He slipped off his shorts and launched himself at his wife, sinking his rigid cock through the golden hairs of her crotch and deep into her gash. Diane gasped as she felt Jeffrey's tool slide deep inside of her until his pubic hair tickled the small brown pucker of her asshole. Her cunt was sopping wet and Jeffrey's tool went all the way in like a hot knife through butter. Diane started sliding back and forth, taking long licks at Karen's cunt, from top to bottom, and at the same time pushing and pulling Jeffrey's prick in and out of her own cunt.

Karen couldn't take it any more. Diane's licking was arousing enough, but Diane also had a crafty little trick of sucking Karen's clit into her mouth, then rolling it around and around and finally biting it gently from top to bottom. Karen was coming, but oh how she ached to have a man's cock deep inside her ravenous gash. Karen squirmed under Diane's continued assault and now she took her own breasts in her hands and started squeezing in rhythm with Diane's licking. Suddenly Karen's body stiffened and she closed her eyes tight shut as she began to come hard. Once she had picked up a lovely black and gold silk kimono at a sale in the city – it was her favourite. She loved the way the gold thread chrysanthemums had been sewn on to the black-as-night background. They always reminded her of the golden starbursts of ecstasy that exploded in the darkness behind her closed lids – just like the ones she was experiencing now.

Meanwhile Jeffrey continued his assault on Diane, who now rested her golden-haired head on Karen's flat belly. Karen just lay there, mellow with post-orgasmic glow, watching the couple fuck through half-closed eyes. Karen could feel Diane's body jolting with each of Jeffrey's thrusts and from the way her stomach muscles were tightening, she knew that Diane was about to come. She looked at Jeffrey and saw him gasping for air like a drowning man; he was about to shoot, too. Karen slid closer to the banging couple, cradling Diane's head in her crotch, and suddenly she felt Diane push back hard against her. Jeffrey gasped as he felt the come shooting out of his cock and deep into Diane's welcoming, clasping pussy.

The trio lay on the floor for a few moments, resting, but fondling each other and getting ready for a second go at each other.

"Don't you think that she and Pete should go at it?" Diane asked her husband.

"It's about time. I think that some of our female guests downstairs are aching for a shot too, but Pete should definitely start off with the best," Jeffrey smiled, cupping and fondling Karen's breasts. "And this is it – present company excepted, of course!"

Karen rose from the floor and slipped out of the remainder of her clothing.

"Why thank you kindly," she said, smiling at her hosts and making a deep curtsey.

"Now don't tempt me," Jeffrey said, and he laughed as he ogled the graceful curves of her body flow and undulate as she bent, "or I'll be banging the hell out of you when my cock has had a chance to recover, and my poor son and heir will never get a shot at you."

"Now come along Jeffrey," Diane said good-naturedly, as she listened to the sounds of the revelry drifting up from the living room downstairs. By the sound of it this was one of the most exciting little parties they'd thrown in quite a while. "Our guests will miss us," Diane repeated as she gently pulled her husband away from Karen. From the little leaps and jerks it was giving, it was plain that his cock was indeed showing signs of 'recovery'.

Karen heard sounds of movement from the next-door room and she walked out into the hallway and paused outside the door to listen. This was Pete's room, she had been told. She took her duties seriously: it was her job to initiate Pete into the mysteries and joys of sex. "Mostly joys," Karen smiled to herself. The door was open a crack and Karen looked in. Pete Lester certainly was a handsome young buck, just as she had heard.

He was about five-foot-eight, but very well muscled and as he walked across the room and turned toward the door Karen could see that he was nude, and had a cock at least as big as his father's.

Karen was about to walk into the room, but she heard some more movement and saw a petite, nicely proportioned girl with short, sandy hair cut in a bob, perhaps a year older than him, walk across the room toward him. Without saying a word, Pete embraced and hugged her, letting his arms snake around her and under the sheer nightie she wore. Karen could see Pete's cock stiffen as he fondled the globes of her ass. Karen leaned against the door and peered in. So Pete needs lessons, does he? she laughed to herself. He seems to be doing just fine with that little cutie, whoever she is.

She continued to watch as Pete raised his arms and lifted the nightie from his playmate in one smooth motion. His stiff cock pressed against the soft, sexy curve of her stomach as they continued in a deep, soul kiss. Karen could see his tongue deep inside his lover's mouth and she saw his hands move up and down her body, slowly and softly. She saw the girl pull away, her long tongue clinging to Pete's mouth as long as possible, and as she pulled away, she sank to her knees and buried her head in Pete's crotch and swallowed his dick, taking it into her mouth in its entirety. Karen could see Pete swaying as his playmate sucked his cock, sliding it in and out of her mouth and, it seemed to Karen who was still watching from the door, deep down into her throat.

Suddenly, the girl pulled Pete's cock from her throat and she could see that Pete was coming. His sticky sweet come squirted out of his cock and all over her firm tits and soft, pale belly as she lay below, catching some in her hands and smearing it over her body. By the time he had finished spurting, the girl's body was shiny and glistening the wetness reflecting the golden light of the bedside lamp. After five or ten minutes of mutual, playful caressing and muttered exchanges that Karen couldn't quite hear, Pete picked her up and lay her across the bed. The girl knew what was coming because she spread her legs and held them aloft, baring a pink, hungry cunt for the final attack. His stamina amazed Karen – his cock had completely recovered after mere minutes of ejaculation. With one swift motion Pete fell on her, burying his larger than average cock deep inside her body. Karen heard her gasp as the shaft drove all the way home.

It was quite a performance. The two rocked back and forth, back and forth, as Pete plunged into her body, in and out, in and out. They rolled over and the girl perched

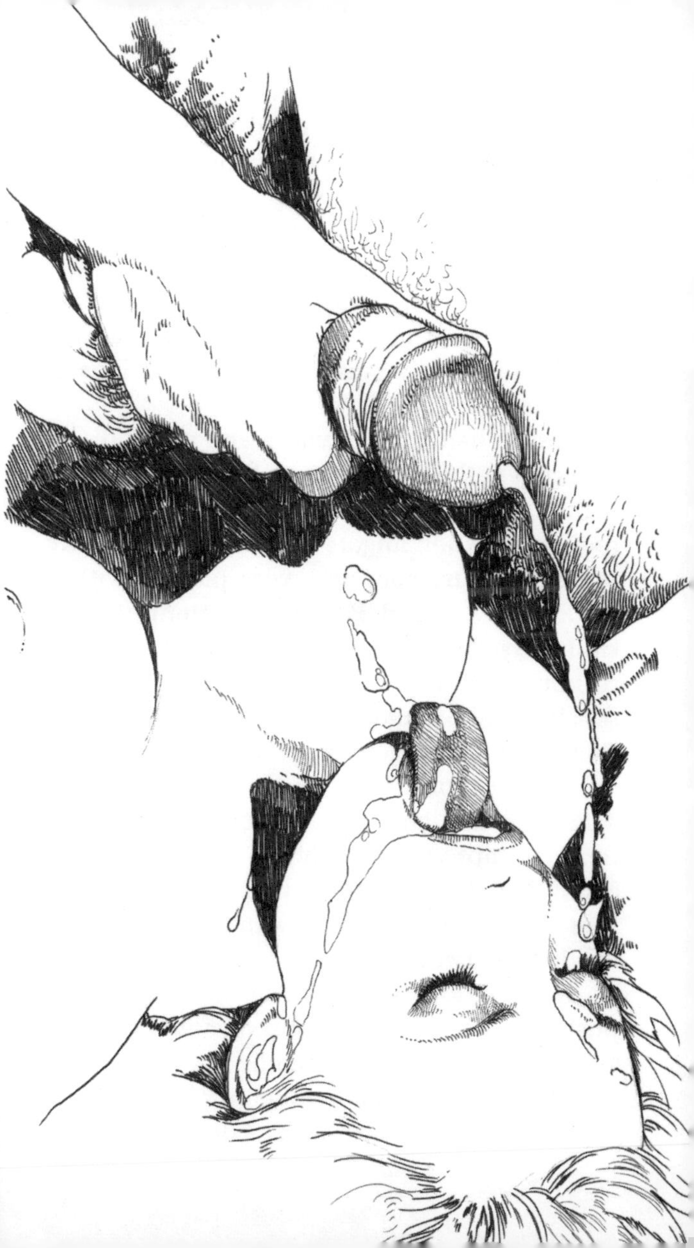

on Pete's body, riding him, like a wild, bucking bronco as he arched his back under her, meeting her downward thrusts with an upward buck, hammering the head of his tool against the roof of her twat, harder and harder until both were gasping, curled and entwined in each others arms. With hardly any warning at all, they both came, panting and gasping for air as the sweet passions of sex overtook them both.

Karen had stayed where she was, quietly drinking in the whole scene. She had to admit – this young stud had excited her. Without realizing it, her fingers had found their way to her pleasure-spot and were playing with it while she watched Pete do his thing. Karen smiled as she saw what had been happening to her body. Her nipples had got hard and sensitive. She longed to play with them, brush them with her fingertips, pinch them between finger and thumb. Her pussy had gotten wet again and the hair that sprouted around her pink cuntlips was already matted; indeed she could feel herself lubricate so much that a thin runnel of juice slowly inched down the inside of her thigh.

Quietly, and still smiling to herself, she pushed the door open and confronted the two young lovers resting on the bed.

"Bravo," she said, laughing. "Really. A splendid performance, Pete. I don't think you need me."

The two were startled and for a moment the girl with the short sandy hair hid under the covers.

"Relax, Robin," Pete said, rising from the bed and moving between them. This must be Karen. "Guess you caught us. You see, this is – uh – my sister Robin, we've been doing it for two years without my parents knowing about it."

"And it sure looks like you've really perfected your act together," said Karen smiling broadly and approaching the young stud she was meant to initiate.

Pete stared at Karen, taking in the gorgeous sight that presented itself. She was almost a head taller than he was and she had the body of a goddess, with large firm breasts and a beautifully sculpted figure. She reached her hand out toward Pete, but before he could take it in his, she dropped her hand onto his penis, which was already stiffening for a third time. Jeez, she thought, this boy's stamina is something else! The sight of Karen Shaw, standing before him nude, hiding not a square inch of her magnificent body had sent the blood racing feverishly through his body. The thought of what he could do, the possibilities that her body presented, had very quickly driven him to a state of pure, unadulterated lust.

She squeezed his organ lightly, and it responded almost immediately, stiffening until it stood erect, at a 90-degree angle. It was still slightly wet from Robin's cunt. Karen held it gently but firmly in her hand, occasionally squeezing or stroking it, feeling the blood as it pulsed and throbbed. Karen glanced over and could see that Robin was watching intently as Karen massaged the marvellous cock. If she was jealous of Karen's ministrations, she showed no sign of it.

Karen felt the juices in her sopping cunt begin to leak through her labia. She needed to fuck this young stud, incestuous girlfriend-sister or not. She stepped closer to Pete and leaned against him, rubbing her breasts against his chest. Karen leaned down and kissed Pete, poking her tongue deep into Pete's mouth wrapping it around his tongue, sucking the saliva from his mouth. She pumped her hand up and down his rod, up and down that slippery weapon, feeling it grow more and more excited and hotter and hotter. She felt his fingers hesitantly probe the thick black bush between her legs, tentatively part the hairs so that he could explore deeper and deeper until he reached the bright pink lips that guarded the entrance to her hot hole – a hole that craved Pete's pole. Suddenly she was amazed to feel herself being picked up. This boy is strong, she thought – really strong! Her long, dark hair trailed behind her as she swung freely in Pete's arms. She felt herself being thrown onto the bed, almost landing atop Robin, who just barely had time to squirm out of the way.

Karen bounced on the bed and found her hands drifting over to Robin, while Pete busied himself by poking his tongue into Karen's twat. My God, Karen thought, Robin has such nice, firm, perky breasts. Robin made no move to resist Karen: far from it, she just lay there enjoying the attention she was getting. Pete shifted around, his legs on either side of Karen's head and his dong hanging tantalizingly over her face. Karen's hands were busy working on Robin, but the urge to suck that cock was overwhelming and she bobbed for it the way she remembered bobbing for apples as a child. Pete's cock was swinging in front of her face and it was covered with a mixture of his own come and Robin's so it was slippery and Karen lifted her head to catch a bite of it as it swung back and forth. God, it tasted good, she thought, as it weaved and dived, and with each swing she lifted her head and tried to catch it in her mouth, but only succeeded in getting a lick. Meanwhile Pete had found her clit and was busily alternately sucking and nibbling at it. The three of them began to roll in a frenzied tangle of arms and legs all around the small bed. In the state we're in, it won't take much to take any of us to cloud number nine, she thought.

Finally, Pete could stand it no more. He shifted positions again, this time pinning Karen beneath him and, once he had located the best angle, thrust in hard. Karen gasped as she felt his cock ram straight into her. It was even bigger than she had thought, and she felt that it was a truly wonderful tight fit. The walls of her cunt were blissfully massaged as he pulled it out and rammed it in, again and again. Karen had gotten so wet with excitement that she could hear the sloshing sound of Pete's prick each time it drove deep into her.

She didn't even know what was happening except that she suddenly felt Robin grab her arm and shove it down between her legs. Robin was using Karen's arm while her brother was banging her. Karen was vaguely aware of the soft silky hair at Robin's cunt and she felt Robin breathing heavily beside her, but all Karen's energies were concentrated on Pete's hard penis hammering away at her pleasure portal without cease, so anything that Robin was doing was for Robin to enjoy all by herself. Sweat coated both their bodies as they lunged against each other, Pete's body slamming down atop Karen's and Karen's rising up to meet each hard, delicious bang as their bodies slapped against each other sending sensations of pleasure racing through their nervous system.

Karen had learned a clever little trick back in the old days, and now she started to use it, and Pete really felt it. Each time he sank his shaft into her, she contracted her cunt muscles, gripping his cock so tight he almost had to struggle to pull it out. She lifted her hips to meet each of his thrusts, and with each thrust she'd press the muscles together, giving his cock the most delicious sensations that he had ever encountered in his short life.

Pete couldn't stand it anymore, and before he knew what was happening he was coming again, shooting his super-heated come into Karen's waiting cavern. The force of his come shooting into her set her off too; she twisted and bucked under him, clutching the buns of his tight, muscular ass as he humped her, almost throwing him on top of his sister who had been masturbating herself with Karen's fingers. The two writhed in uncontrollable ecstasy, abandoning themselves entirely to their orgasmic bliss. When they both calmed down, Pete was amazed to feel Karen's finger deeply implanted in his asshole. Just before his crisis and her own, she had slipped her slim digit into the sweaty crack between his hard, wildly-jerking ass-cheeks, located his tight sphincter and thrust in. In the heat of the moment it was just one sensation among so many, and he had hardly noticed the sexy intrusion. Only now could he luxuriate in the feeling of her long finger slowly withdrawing, giving a sassy wiggle as it went, causing his cock to give a final, weak spurt over her sex as it, too, withdrew.

At last he rolled off of her and she could feel a little rush of semen cascade from the mouth of her stretched vaginal cave. Karen's cunt was sopping wet and a small puddle formed between her legs and soaked into the bed sheets. Before she had time to rest, Karen heard the door open and in walked Jeffrey and Diane, a joint in each of their hands and laughing like mad.

"Well, this makes a pretty picture," said Diane, her laughter making her breasts jiggle prettily as she passed them each a joint. "It's like – the family that fucks together, comes together."

Jeffrey was equally stoned and both he and Diane climbed clumsily into bed with their son and daughter. It took more than this to shock or faze Karen, but somehow she felt her presence was superfluous and slipped out of bed and headed for the door. By the time she got there and turned around, the stoned parents were well on their way to fucking their own offspring. Jeffrey had a mouthful of Robin's breasts and Diane was sucking on Pete's limp tool. It'll be a while before she gets any joy out of that particular cock, thought Karen with some satisfaction.

Bemused by the display of overt incest and not really knowing whether she approved or disapproved, Karen just shook her head and went to look for a shower. She was thoroughly sweaty, and though she had been fucked properly several times, her body was still craving more. This had just been an appetizer, and before the evening was over she would not only need more, but she would get it, too.

She found the shower and stepped into it, turning the hot water on full and letting the sharp needle spray dig deep into the pores of her skin. The sweat rinsed off, but her pussy still leaked young Pete's abundant sperm. She angled the shower head to give herself an impromptu douche. She loved the cleansing process that transformed her from tired, sweaty orgiast to sparklingly clean, revitalised Amazon, ready to do battle with any cock or cunt that came her way. The water felt so good running in scalding rivulets down over the gentle curves and slopes of her tits and belly, converging so that it streamed through her pubic bush, reawakening, redoubling her sexual hungers. She abandoned herself to the hot water until she felt her entire body tingle and glow.

Karen turned the water off and stepped

out of the shower. She looked at the full-length mirror on the wall facing her and surveyed her body. Her breasts were large and firm and rode high on her chest. There was no sag and she grinned to herself as she remembered only the other day winning 'the pencil test' – when a group of them had passed a pencil around the girls to see if it could be captured under a breast. Not in her case. Her nipples were large and circular and red as cherries. Her body was sleek and well shaped and her hips were round and beautifully proportioned. She started drying herself but continued watching her body in the mirror. Her breasts jiggled slightly from the drying movement. The patch of black hair between her legs was almost a perfect "V" and it was dense and curly, completely hiding the pink cuntlips that now ached for more. Oh yes, she thought, suddenly remembering Paul, the big, handsome stud who had opened the door for her. Her mind cast back to the growing bulge in his briefs and, at that moment, she actually licked her lips.

As if by some form of weird telepathy, Paul had been wandering in the direction of the bathroom, but instead of walking in he watched from the doorway as Karen continued surveying her body and very sensuously drying herself.

"Here, let me do that," he said suddenly,

startling Karen.

He took the towel from her hands just as she was about to dry her breasts. Paul was also nude and he pressed his body against hers as he put his mouth to her lips and give her a deep, open-mouthed kiss. Karen could feel his massive cock stiffen and press against her wet body as he rubbed against her and probed with his tongue deep in her mouth. Karen gasped as she felt his tongue deep in her mouth. She almost had difficulty in breathing, but she didn't want him to stop either.

Finally, Paul pulled away from her and swept her off her feet and, before she could protest, carried her into one of the bedrooms and tossed her half-way across the room and onto a bed. He lunged across the room at her body, but Karen, horny as she was for his bulging cock, was feeling playful and jumped out of his way. Paul wound up on an empty, but wet, sheet for Karen was still sopping wet. Karen danced across the room and stood facing Paul, she wiggled her hips at him, goading him, enticing him. He lay on the bed staring at her.

"Come and get it," she laughed, wiggling her hips once again, this time burying her hands into the bush of black hair guarding her cunt and pulled it apart for Paul to see. She revealed the juicy pink lips of her cunt peeking through the bush and this was more than Paul could stand. He rolled off the bed and lunged forward again trying to get a handful of the elusive bombshell that lured him on. But again Karen slithered out of his grasp.

"Follow me, follow me," Karen sang as she danced back and forth in front of the sprawled figure of Paul.

Chapter 4

"Follow me, follow me," Karen continued to sing as she danced about, her lush body squirming seductively. Paul dragged himself off the floor and followed the dancing figure. He could see her now, doing chin-ups from the top of the doorpost. She must be very strong, Paul thought to himself as he watched her strain to lift her body. Her breasts tightened and it looked like her nipples would pop right off those big, bouncing boobs. She spread her legs and swung back and forth, and as Paul, made another dash for her, she dropped to the ground and whirled into the room.

Now Paul could see where she had been leading him. Off in a corner of the large room there was a waterbed, and when Karen jumped on to it with a little scream of pleasure, it started undulating as if it had a life of its own.

Karen was flat on the bed and still it continued sloshing about, pushing one part of her body up and out while another part of her body sank beneath the waves. It was almost as if the waterbed was saying, "here – take her breasts! No, look – take her cunt! No, look here – take her thighs and belly!"

Now Karen was ready, and Paul knew it. From the doorway he could see the thick growth of black pubic hair outlined against the silver of the satin sheets, like the bull's-eye in a target. Paul bounded into the room and leaped onto the waterbed, setting it in motion again. Karen's ass bounded up and down on the waves of the waterbed. Paul kneeled between her legs and buried his head between her thighs. Finally he would get his revenge for Karen's cock teasing performance. He opened his mouth wide and stuck his tongue through the thick bush, pushing through it until he could feel the little pink clit at the top of her pussy. He took it between his teeth and bit gently. Karen gasped as the near-pain raced through her body, but the sensation was short-lived and it was soon replaced by one of pleasure as her aching clit was being chewed and sucked around and around in Paul's mouth as now he shielded his teeth behind his nibbling lips.

He reached up for her body, his fingers roughly probing her torso until he reached her breasts. Now he had a handful of what he wanted. Her breasts were full and firm, and they responded instantly to his touch. He gripped her nipples between his fingers and rolled the nipples back and forth, pinching them hard. Again, the sharp sensation made Karen gasp, but the feelings of pleasure soon overtook the pain. He handled her breasts roughly, pinching and slapping them, but that was what she needed. Karen pushed her hips against Paul's face, as if trying to engulf his entire head in her hot, wet cunt. She spread her hips wider and wider, lifting her legs and almost doing a split. Her cunt opened into a gaping hole and Paul pushed his face hard against it. His tongue probed far into her vaginal canal, rolling back and forth, probing as far as its roots would allow. Karen was going mad with passion. She had come just a few minutes ago but under Paul's intense assault her body was aching with pleasure. Her entire body felt like it would melt as she writhed and squirmed, trying now to grapple Paul's entire body between her strong, straining legs.

Paul had never tasted, a cunt like this one before. Karen virtually gushed her sweet come and he felt like he was drowning in a sea of honey. The soft curls of Karen's pubic bush rubbed back and forth across Paul's face as he licked and she squirmed. At last he could stand it no more. His cock had grown to full size and her thrashing body aroused him like he'd never been aroused before. His cock ached to sink into the sweet honey pot that he'd been licking.

"Suck me, suck me more," Karen breathed between gasps of sweet ecstasy. "Oh God, chew me, bite me."

"Uh-unh," Paul panted, as he pulled his mouth from her slit. "Now I'm going to fuck the hell out of you, my pretty."

"Well, fucking do it, man, just do it!" Karen screamed.

Karen looked up as Paul straightened up. He had one of the biggest cocks she'd ever seen. This one, besides giving her a massive orgasm, might just kill her, she thought, but at least she'd die happy. Karen spread her legs and licked her lips in anticipation. She took a deep breath knowing that once Paul shoved his massive tool into her slit she would blast into orbit. Paul fell forward scoring almost a direct hit on her cunt. In one swift, simple motion his cock rammed deep into her cunt, tearing through her black bush and plunging past the pink lips until it was so deep inside her vagina that its rubbery glans nudged her cervix. God! It was as if she could almost feel the tip of Paul's cock poking against the tip of her spine!

The motion of the waterbed moved them

both back and forth, rubbing Paul's cock against Karen's swollen cunt lips. Before Paul's cock had made two or three strokes Karen felt waves of heat spreading through her entire body. She was coming and she could feel Paul's cock swelling up prior to ejaculating its massive load of sperm into her waiting hole. She arched her back, pushing her pelvis against Paul's and grinding back and forth as Paul pushed in and out. Karen raked her fingernails lightly across Paul's back. She was rapidly blacking out from the overwhelming sensation of his banging. Before she knew what she was doing she dug her nails deep into Paul's back and almost totally blacked out. She was only vaguely aware that she was coming and only vaguely aware that Paul had started to come shooting his boiling load into her hole. Only one sound escaped her almost paralyzed lips: *"Ohhhhh..."*

Paul rolled off Karen and plopped onto the waterbed setting it in motion again. Karen opened her eyes and smiled at Paul. She surveyed her own body noting that her upper chest was still pink from the excitement and that her cunt ached. She reached over to touch Paul and brushed her hand against his cock. It was still erect, and Paul was smiling.

"Ready for more, lover boy?" Karen smiled, rubbing her hand up and down the cock which had almost murdered her.

"Can you take it, sweet bitch?" He smiled, reaching his arm under her and flipping her over on her stomach.

"This is what I want," Paul said running his finger lightly down Karen's back, down the small of her back and through the lovely, peach-coloured split of her ass and down to the tight little tan pucker ringed with muscle.

"No, you're too big," Karen protested squirming slightly, but it was too late. Paul had already gotten to his knees and pulled her legs apart and kneeled between her open legs.

Karen struggled against Paul, but she wasted her efforts because the motion of the waterbed made it impossible for her to rise. Paul had his hands on both of her firm, peach buttocks and was leaning hard on them.

"No, uhhh, no," Karen gasped as she felt Paul's hands spreading her cheeks. She could feel the cool air on the ring of muscles that surrounded her asshole.

"I'm going to cornhole you good," Paul breathed as he bent over and kissed her sweet asshole. He licked it with his tongue, lubricating and thoroughly wetting the tight knob of muscles so he could slip in easier. Karen was panting, still trying to squirm away from Paul but it was no use. His hands were firmly planted on her ass and there was nothing she could do. Suddenly, without realizing what was happening, she felt pressure at her asshole. The giant dong, which had just recently reamed her cunt so thoroughly, was now at the gate and pressing hard. It hurt slightly, but Karen nevertheless stopped fighting Paul and relaxed her ass, resisting a natural defensive instinct to tighten her sphincter against his assault. Paul's cock was still wet from the previous fucking, glistening and covered with a mixture of both his and Karen's come, and now it slipped easily into her tight little asshole.

Suddenly her hole was spread wide as Paul's thick cock slipped quickly into the forbidden portal. The burst of pain that accompanied Paul's massive intrusion deep into her bowels soon vanished and now she could feel his warm, slippery cock moving back and forth inside of her and massaging her tingly nerves that lined the anal passage. Karen couldn't believe it, but she was beginning to get really turned on. Paul slipped his hands under her body and cupped her breasts in his hands, letting the nipples slip through his fingers, pinching them as he undulated on top of her. The waterbed pushed her firm buttocks up to meet each thrust of his cock and he went deeper and deeper into her ass, and Karen loved every minute of it. Her breathing fell into a regular pattern and she could feel the blood rushing through her body, setting her

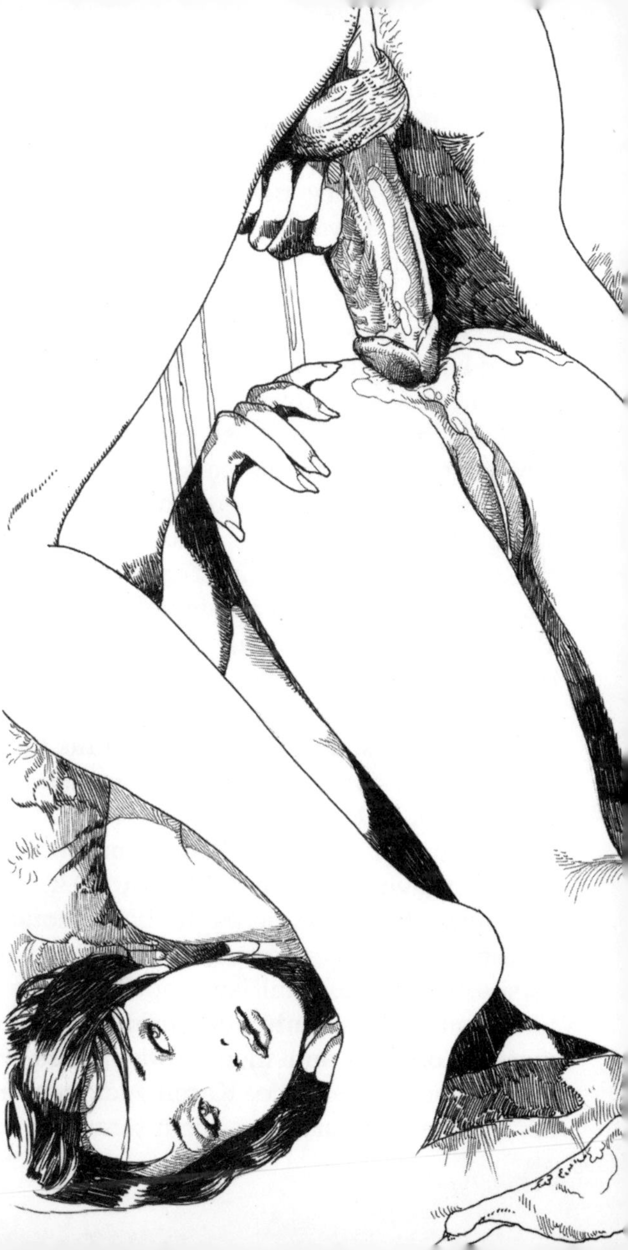

nerves on fire.

Paul felt her responding and continued his in-and-out, in-and-out motion. Her ass muscles were very tightly wrapped around his tool, and it was growing tender and red from the rubbing it was getting but Paul didn't care. Karen had now overcome her reluctance and was feeling glad that Paul had forced his cock into her ass. She really needed this and now she moved her body in rhythm with his, pushing her ass up to meet the downward thrust of his cock and absorbing it as deep into her as she could. Karen could swear that his cock was almost poking into her stomach, but she didn't care because it just felt so fuckin' good and funky. Meanwhile Paul's cock was beginning to overheat. It felt sore and tender and before he knew what was happening he felt a tickle in his balls and then a preliminary squirt from the tip of his penis and then the dam broke and he spurted it all into the hot little asshole he was reaming.

Karen was glad that Paul came because she was having trouble holding it back, too. But now she surrendered to her emotions and she felt shudders racing through her body as she too, came. Paul lay atop Karen for a few moments, silently recovering from his massive orgasm and then slowly pulled his weapon out of her hole. Karen suddenly felt her asshole chill and felt a slight soreness, but she felt very sleepy and as Paul rose to leave her, she rolled over and surrendered to the weariness that was overtaking her.

Even in her sleep Karen could feel the slight discomfort of her asshole, and now her mind drifted back to the first time she had been cornholed. It had all started innocently enough when she was shopping at a department store. She was wandering through the lingerie section when she noticed a short, beautifully-built blonde. Almost immediately, Karen felt turned on and walked toward the blonde and stood next to her, also looking at the lingerie on the counter. The two talked for a few moments and Karen was hoping desperately that she could find a way to get to know this woman better, to meet her a second time and to lure her into bed.

"I'm tired of shopping," the blonde said suddenly. "Why don't we have some coffee at my place?"

Karen couldn't believe her ears. She was trying vainly to find some way to make a pass at this little bombshell with the large breasts and slinky walk and suddenly the roles had been reversed.

"Okay, sure! That would be nice!" Karen nodded, smiling brightly, yet trying not to seem too eager.

As the blonde smiled back at her there was a certain look in her eye – a look of pure, predatory, sexual hunger, and Karen knew that they were on the same wavelength, but neither of them said a word. It turned out to be a short cab ride to the luxury building where the blonde lived and she gave the handsome young doorman an unusually big smile as she led Karen into the building.

"Make yourself comfortable," the blonde said as she led Karen into the apartment. "I'll only be a minute."

Karen pulled her coat off and kicked her shoes off and curled up on the couch. This certainly was an expensive apartment she thought as she glanced around at the rich furnishings and deep carpet. Karen tucked her legs under her, letting her skirt slide up her thighs and she leaned back against the couch, her breasts pushing against her sweater. Karen's message was abundantly clear and so were her large, firm breasts straining against the fabric that barely concealed them.

Karen's message must have been well received because the blonde, who hadn't even introduced herself yet, returned with the coffee. But in addition to the coffee she had found time to get out of most of her clothing and appeared wearing nothing more than a string bikini.

"I just hate being dressed all the time," she smiled. "It's so confining and the minute I get into the house I usually strip completely.

I'm just wearing this because you're here."

Karen could scarcely believe her eyes. Those big round breasts that had caught her eye were for real and were straining against the sheer silk of the bikini top. The rest of her body was firm and fleshy, just the way Karen liked it, and Karen could see that the lovely bombshell had shaved her pussyhair because there was none of it curling around the skimpy bundle of fabric that barely covered her crotch. And Karen could see the outline of large, firm cuntlips pushing against the slender silk of the triangle.

"Don't dress up on account of me," Karen smiled, continuing to survey the luscious body. "I know exactly how you feel, I like wandering around naked too, so please don't wear that just for me."

"You're too kind," Karen's new friend smiled. "But you go ahead and undress first. You're wearing more than I am."

This proposition made sense to Karen, who was pleased with the way the afternoon was turning out. She had set out to seduce a total stranger and instead wound up at the stranger's home, being seduced herself. Not bad.

"Okay," Karen smiled, reasoning that the outfit her hostess was wearing hid almost nothing, so she was pretty much nude anyway. Karen uncoiled her body from the couch and walked toward her seducer who had already set down the tray of coffee and had curled up in an armchair, her arms crossed under her breasts pushing them even higher. She stopped about four feet from her new friend and without any warning or prelude simply pulled her sweater over the top of her head in one smooth motion. Karen's hair danced and her breasts quivered cutely from the sudden motion, but the move had its intended effect. The blonde suddenly sat up and stared in wide-eyed amazement at Karen's boobs, delighted by their size and perfect shape. Karen enjoyed the attention she was getting and she swung her hips slightly to keep her breasts jiggling. She lifted her arms to the waistband of her microskirt and rolled it down slightly, revealing her lovely navel and then the slight swelling of her stomach and then further still past the bikini-brief undies she wore, letting her skirt fall to the floor. Karen stepped away from the skirt and she could see that her new friend's eyes were following her very closely indeed.

Karen was wearing a bikini-brief panty that was virtually transparent and her big, thick thatch of cunt hair was plain to see. In fact a couple of her thick public hairs had even poked through the flimsy material of the panty. She rolled the panty downward, finally revealing her lush bush and she could see that her friend's eyes had opened so wide that they were almost ready to pop out of her head.

Karen drew herself up to her full height and did a slight, quick pirouette. She just adored showing off her body, especially when her audience was this interested.

"It's your turn, darling," Karen smiled, as she fell back toward the couch, her legs apart and her hips pushed forward showing off her cunt.

"Yes, my turn," her short, blonde friend smiled. "I don't think I can match *that* performance, though."

The blonde was entirely different than Karen. Her shorter body had an entirely different structure, but it was no less exciting than Karen's and Karen sat back to watch her friend strip the few remaining bits of silk from her lovely form. The blonde took a deep breath and it looked like the string-top would almost snap as her breasts spread out further and further, but somehow the top managed to contain the massive boobs. She reached her hands behind her, and again the breasts started their outward expansion, but this time, she untied the bow behind her neck and the top practically flew off, revealing superb breasts with large, half-dollar-sized areolas whose nipples were a luscious light brown.

The blonde turned around and for the first time Karen got a good look at her firm, round bottom that was one of the things that had first attracted Karen to this gorgeous, lively creature in the department store. With one hand on either hip she slowly rolled the triangle-shaped bottom of the swimsuit off her hips, revealing smooth, perfectly formed skin and the brown cluster of muscles that formed her asshole. In one swift motion, the blonde turned around setting her breasts in motion and revealing the full front view which showed a lovely little round bulge above the tummy and two pink cuntlips completely shaved of all the hair around them.

"Do you recognize me now?" The blonde said to Karen as she stood nude and sensuous before her.

"No, I don't think I do," Karen said, continuing to study the lovely bitch that stood before her, but studying her for two reasons now: because she was a big turn on and because now she was trying to place both the face and the body.

"But wait, there's something familiar," Karen continued, stretching on the couch and pointing both her breasts at the woman she continued to fail to recognize.

"Do you remember the orgy at the teacher's house at Elm Street High?" She smiled, twitching her breasts in response to Karen's message.

"NANCY!!!" Karen almost shrieked,

jumping up from the couch. "Nancy, is that you?"

"Yes it is, and I recognized you way back at the department store, you silly bitch," she said, spreading her arms wide open in welcome.

Yeah, well, you're a blonde now, thought Karen. Not like you were back then.

Karen rushed to her friend and they embraced for the first time in almost seven years. Karen almost scooped Nancy up in her arms and hugged her. Their breasts rubbed against each other and they dug their fingernails into each other's backs. Those Saturday afternoon orgies with their gym teacher and her husband had taught them much about sex and as they embraced and thoughts of those magic sessions came back to them, they started getting aroused. Their nipples hardened and contracted and the rubbing of Nancy's bare cunt against Karen's thick bush got Nancy's clitoris erect and standing at attention in no time.

Before either of the women, old friends who were reunited only because of a casual pickup, knew what was happening they were rolling around on the thick pile rug, over and over. Each one wanted to give the other one interminable pleasure and they were in such a rush that they just rolled aimlessly, grabbing a boob here, a handful of cunt there or a fistful of ass.

Karen was bigger and stronger than Nancy, and after a few minutes of helpless giggling and rolling around, she managed to get Nancy on the floor with her legs spread wide open. Karen got a giant mouthful of Nancy's lovely, bare cunt and started chewing, while she reached up with her long, slender arms and grabbed a healthy fistful of each boob.

There was no hair to tickle Karen as she slurped and sucked vigorously on Nancy's cunt and she had nothing but pure pleasure. The high firm cuntlips, the hard, round clit and the sugary sweet juice that flowed from her pussy. And that wasn't all. Nancy's breasts stood high and shapely on her body, but they were nevertheless as soft as down pillows, with large nipples that contracted and were as hard and pointed as bullets. Fingering Nancy's nipples was driving Karen wild. She could feel her own gash itching and aching for the kind of treatment she was giving Nancy.

Nancy, too, was practically going into orbit. It had been a long time since she'd gotten this thorough a working over and she squirmed against the rug, feeling its shag pile rough against her back as she felt Karen gnawing at her cunt and tearing at her breasts. Nancy tried to hold off, but it was to no avail. Usually she could contain herself, but now she couldn't. Karen's chewing and her hands were pushing her way over the brink of control and finally she surrendered, letting her orgasm flood through her body. It was one of the most violent orgasms she'd ever had. Nancy bucked and twisted as the nerves in her body went haywire. Karen couldn't hold on and found herself thrown onto the deep shag carpet as Nancy twisted and bucked.

"*Ohmygod, ohmygod!*" was all that Nancy could say over and over again, as she writhed on the floor. Karen sat up and watched as her high school friend and lover suffered the torment of orgasm, until finally Nancy collapsed to the ground, breathing heavily, sweat running in rivulets in the valley between her breasts and down toward her cunt.

"*God,* I needed that," Nancy said at last, regaining her breath and propping herself up on one arm. "Now it's *your* turn, my love."

"I was kind of hoping you'd get around to doing me," Karen smiled, cupping her breasts in her hand and offering them to Nancy, who now got up, took a pillow from the couch and tossed it to the center of the living room.

"Put your ass right there, lover," Nancy whispered to Karen. "Get it nice and high, so I can reach into your honeypot and suck you dry."

Karen rose to all fours, and like the slinkiest and sexiest of cats made her way to the pillow. Nancy stood over her hands on her hips, legs wide apart and breasts quivering slightly in anticipation. Karen, always a tease, moved ever so slowly, keeping one eye on Nancy to make sure that Nancy was enjoying the seductive little act.

Karen finally reached the pillow and flopped over on her back, her ass dead centre on the pillow. She threw her long dark hair behind her and it spread across the carpet like a rich, black sunburst. She wiggled on the pillow to dig her ass into it, setting her breasts quivering. Nancy smiled and sank to all fours just as Karen had down and now crawled over to her.

"*Grrrowll,*" she breathed.

"*Mmmmeww,*" Karen responded, lifting her hips and pushing the mound of flesh, hidden beneath its thick bush at Nancy.

"*Grrowwll,*" Nancy breathed again, sniffing the delicate, intoxicating odour of Karen's pussy, which was still slightly wet as a result of Karen's working over of Nancy. "Open wide, wider..."

Karen squirmed against the rug she lay on, feeling her skin covered with gooseflesh as the pile dug in. Obediently, she opened her legs as far as she could, almost doing a split. Nancy watched in amazement as Karen's legs spread farther and farther, and then as Karen lifted them, it looked almost as if Karen's cunt had come alive and was, perversely, going to suck at Nancy's mouth, rather than the other way around. It was more than Nancy could take and without another word she opened her mouth and pulled her lips back and sank her head into the hair-covered V between Karen's legs, scoring a direct hit on her already erect clit, that almost poked through the dense bush. Nancy opened her mouth as wide as she could and sucked in all of Karen's cunt as she could including the long silky hair that shielded it. The hair felt funny in her mouth, but the sweet ooze that she was sucking out of Karen's cunt more than made up for it. Nancy's arms weren't quite as long as Karen's but still she had no trouble at all getting a firm grip on Karen's boobs pushing and squeezing them around, gripping the nipples and then letting them slip very slowly from her grasp, gripping them again and letting them slip very slowly from her grasp once more, then repeating the whole trick.

The blood rushed madly through Karen's body giving her skin a very warm glow. Karen moaned softly as now Nancy transferred her attentions from the breasts to the hair-pie between Karen's legs, pulling the hair clear of Karen's slit and then digging her tongue deep, deep into it, trying to poke against the back wall and sucking every bit of juice out of Karen's aching cunt. Karen, who had dreamed of this happening to her when she had being doing the same to Nancy only a few minutes ago, was no longer on the planet Earth. She had gone into orbit a long time ago, had closed her eyes and no longer understood what was happening to her except that whatever it was she liked it very, very much. Nancy, ever the artist, transferred her attentions back and forth from cunt to boobs, from slit to knockers, playing, teasing, pinching, biting, hurting, over and over again, varying her actions so that Karen's body, writhing against the shag of the rug, couldn't get used to any sort of routine. And Karen loved it. One moment the sucking would drive her wild, the next it would be the pinching and then the biting and then the scratching. Karen buried her hands deep into the rug, trying to hold back, hold back so she could enjoy it longer, hold back so that Nancy would keep playing with her forever, sucking, pinching, pulling and biting, over and over again.

But it was no use. Nancy was a touch mistress and she wanted to bring Karen off and Karen was powerless to resist, eventually succumbing and having to surrender completely and let the waves of orgasm wash through her entire body. The ceiling that Karen was staring at started swirling around and around. Suddenly her cunt tingled in the most delicious way imaginable and her breasts entire body went stiff and then slack, stiff and slack again and again. Her breasts quivered and her legs moved jerkily as she dug her fingers deeper and deeper into the carpet and let the orgasm assume control of her body.

Karen took a long time in returning to earth. There was a commotion going on around her, but she was still in her own little capsule, her own private bubble of existence.

Gradually she became more conscious of what was happening around her. She was vaguely aware of the handsome black doorman, Danny, as she heard Nancy calling him. He wasn't wearing his uniform anymore, in fact he wasn't wearing anything anymore. Karen was pretty sure of that because she could see his big, stiff cock, bigger than anything she'd ever seen before, and it was heading straight into Nancy's twat, without pausing, without foreplay, his dong soared straight into her hole and Karen could hear Nancy gasp as it pushed past her cuntlips and banged against the back of her gash. She could hear the slap-slap of their bodies as Danny slammed his firm, muscled body against the soft, white flesh of Nancy under him, again and again, until

Orgy Girl ★ 93

Nancy gasped in pain.

"Stop, oh please *stop*," she panted between slaps of their bodies, but Danny kept it up.

"Keep going Danny, don't let the bitch quit now," Karen heard another voice say. She glanced around and saw another man, this one tall, thin and white with a long bullwhip in his hands.

"Oh please, Keith, tell Danny to stop, please, please," Nancy cried.

Karen feared for her friend and tried to get to her feet but she heard a whizzing sound and yelped in pain as the whip snaked out and wrapped itself around her ankle.

"Back on the floor, lesbian bitch," Keith bellowed at Karen, who now wondered what she had gotten into.

"Okay, Danny, let her up, but tie her across that couch for a little punishment, then well get to this one here," Keith laughed.

Karen made a slight move and the whip flicked out again, this time coming so close to her that she could feel the air moving.

"Hold still bitch," Keith spat out.

Karen turned and could see that Danny had withdrawn from Nancy, but he was coming and shooting it out all over her body in great gobs and streams. He picked her up and laid her across the back of the couch and shackled her hand and foot so she couldn't move. Danny walked over to Karen and plopped down beside her and ran his fingers through her hair. Karen, startled, recoiled.

"Don't worry baby, this is a little game they play a couple of times a month," he whispered to her. "Keith digs it, Nancy digs it and so do I. Now why don't you relax."

Nancy could barely move. But she turned her head toward Karen and smiled as Danny put his arm around Karen's back and cupped one of her boobs in his strong hands.

Now Keith stripped his shorts off, showing off his erection that stood just as stiffly as Danny's did, though his cock was smaller and more slender. He drew his whip back and brought it forward sharply across Nancy's buttocks. Nancy yelped as the pain raced through her body.

"Take that you lesbian bitch," he spat out at her and brought the whip forward again, this time an inch or two higher, creating another ugly red welt in Nancy's white backside.

"Oh please stop, please stop, I'll be faithful," Nancy pleaded. "Just stop, never again, never again – "

But the whip came forward again, sharply this time, landing across the first welt and raising it even higher.

Nancy was reduced to wailing and tears, gasping, barely able to talk. Keith laughed as he raised the whip a second time, and a third time and again and again. Karen made a move as if to jump up, but Danny grabbed her and restrained her.

"Look, they both dig this," he hissed as Karen, looking at her body and licking his lips. He pushed Karen down on her back and covered her body with his, grabbing her boobs and pressing them down into her ribs. Karen could feel his big cock stiffen, and she felt him slide up, still pinning her breasts. He pushed his cock roughly in her face and as Karen gasped trying to breathe he shoved it into her mouth almost choking her. He pumped his cock in and out of her mouth, while in the background, Karen heard Keith cursing, the whip cracking and Nancy screaming and wailing.

Karen was going out of her mind, but his goddamn cock tasted good. She could still taste the residue of his come and now she felt a new trickle. She gasped for air and kept swallowing it as it trickled. It tasted sweet and she didn't want to lose a drop of it. Suddenly Danny pulled his cock from her mouth and slid down her body, treating her breasts roughly. He pulled her legs apart and shoved his dong deep into her gash. Karen's cunt felt good from the treatment Nancy had given it, but it felt even better now with a real cock inside of it reaming the hell out of her.

It only took two minutes and she was coming again, bucking and twisting under

Danny as he released his own load and let it shoot deep into her. Suddenly Danny turned over, getting on the floor with Karen atop him. This was going to be a new treat for Karen, now completely unconcerned about what was happening to her masochistic girlfriend. She rode up and down, up and down on Danny's rod, pumping furiously and feeling her cunt being pummelled by his massive tool. Suddenly she became aware of Keith hunching over her.

"So you're not a lezzie after all," he whispered. "You just wanted to hump my wife, you bitch."

Karen was suddenly rather frightened by the proximity of this lunatic sadist, and tried to get off Danny, but he had his arms locked around her and his legs were wrapped around hers, spreading them and holding them down.

"Now, you're going to get it right up your ass," Keith whispered with an evil smile on his face. "Right up your ass, for stealing my wife, you big dyke bitch."

"No, no, please," she pleaded, but it was no use. Danny had her in a strong, tight grip, his cock still inside her, and she was powerless to move. Keith crouched between Karen's spread legs being held down by Danny and placed his cock against the damp brown star of her little asshole.

"Take that, you little bitch," he breathed as he leaned forward slightly pushing his cock into the ring of muscles and then past them so that the head of his cock popped into her rectal cave.

"No, *stop*," Karen gasped as her resisting, protesting muscular rings screamed at the determined invasion. She could feel an extreme discomfort, bordering on actual pain, shooting through her entire anal region as Keith's cock pushed relentlessly further and further into her asshole.

"No, stop," she panted again, not really meaning it this time as the discomfort transformed into exquisite pleasure. Now Karen was being reamed from both sides and she was beginning to enjoy it. A big black stud under her and a white rider atop of her. For the next five minutes she revelled in the extraordinary, novel sensation of being 'sandwiched'. The big men were moving like a piston engine now and Karen loved it. She had already come about a half dozen times, but now she felt both her lovers pouring forth their magic love potions and both her cunt and asshole clasped tenderly as the juice poured into both her orifices.

Nancy had gotten free from her shackles and now walked over to the threesome, lying exhausted on the floor. She stood over them, hands on her hips, legs apart smiling down at

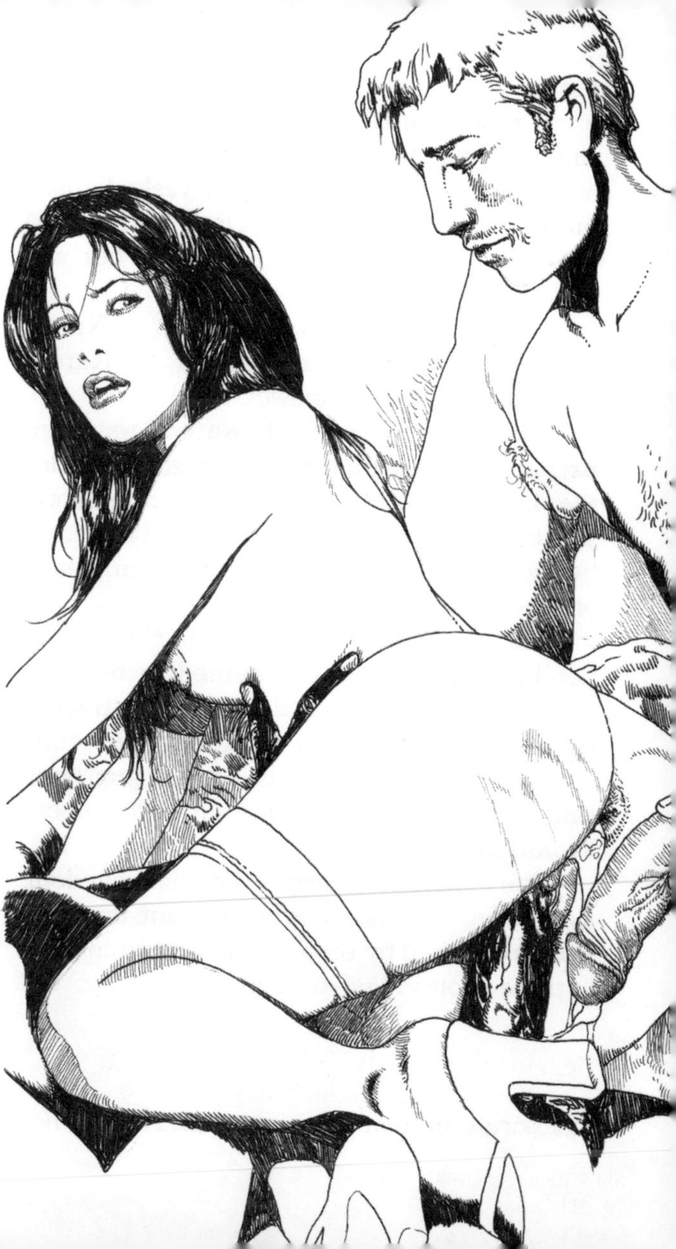

them.

"I hope you enjoyed out little game," she smiled down at Karen. "I always do."

Karen who had now been fucked more thoroughly than she had in a long time smiled up, "Yeah, once I get the hang of it, but you had me going there for a while."

"Surprises are always better," Nancy smiled, reaching a hand down to Karen. "C'mon, let's take a shower."

The two women showered together, exchanging more than just casual gropes under the hot water. Both had been completely satisfied, in fact, pretty much fucked to death, but somehow they just seemed to turn each other on more and more.

Karen spent that night with Nancy and her husband, but Keith seemed to be tired so Nancy and Karen cuddled up. Both were too sore to try anything heavy, but they slept in each other's arms, exchanging deep soul kisses, until they both fell into a deep, exhausted slumber.

The experience, despite having a big dong shoved up her ass, was a pleasant one and Karen dropped by several times more to have both her holes filled at once.

* * *

Memories of that evening with Nancy, her

husband and Danny were almost as pleasant as the real thing, but now the gentle rocking of the waterbed she had been dozing on was slowly bringing Karen back to the real world.

Chapter 5

The waterbed started undulating softly and its wave motion gently awakened Karen. She was suddenly aware of other people in the room, over across the room she could see three bodies close together lovingly caressing one another. Karen could only get a partial view of things through the one eye that she had tentatively opened and that view was distorted by the up and down motion of the waterbed. Karen opened her other eye and looked more closely at the trio in the corner.

Now she could see the petite Robin, who had joined Karen and Pete for a tumble in the sack, kneeling before another woman. The woman was none other than Diane, the hostess of this little bash and Robin's mother. Robin was kneeling in front of Diane who was sitting on a beanbag chair with her legs wide apart and her ringlets of golden cunt hair surrounded her hole. Karen felt a warmth between her legs as she viewed Diane's crotch, the golden hair thin enough to let the pink lips of her cunt and her reddish clit show. But even more than Diane's cunt, her small, oval tits, so small that her areolas practically covered the entire tits, jiggled up and down as she squirmed deeper into the beanbag. Robin was breathing hard on the floor in front of her mother, watching as Diane took her own tits in her hands and squeezed them gently, cupping them and offering them to Robin, her daughter.

"Here, baby, take them," Diane cooed. "You probably don't remember the last time you sucked on them."

"I was pretty small then," Robin giggled as she climbed up her mother's body, sensuously pausing to run her tits through her mother's cunt hair.

"Ohhhh!" Robin breathed as her tits rubbed through the curly golden hair. Now she slithered further up her body and sucked her mother's tits into her mouth. The tits may have been small, but they filled Robin's mouth adequately and she murmured with delight as the nipples hardened and slithered about around her tongue, through her teeth and over her lips. Watching from the waterbed, Karen could see the saliva dribbling out of Robin's mouth and down her mother's body, mingling with the sweat to form little pools in the creases of her skin and navel.

"Go down on me, baby girl," Diane breathed. "Suck my cunt, little girl, oh, please, suck it."

Diane squirmed harder and harder, burying her ass deeper and deeper into the beanbag chair, so that Robin had to wriggle all the way down, her head in her mother's crotch and her ass up in the air so that she could get her mouth down over her mother's gold-fringed cunt. Karen lay on the waterbed letting the wave motions move her up and down slowly, watching Robin's ass. It was a lovely ass and Karen felt the warmth spread through her body just watching it waggle as Robin bit and sucked on her mother's writhing body.

Robin's body hair had not yet grown in fully and Karen could see Robin's bright pink gash through the downy dark blonde hair that sprouted around it. Karen wished she had the energy to get up and go over there and get a mouthful of it, but she just didn't feel like moving so she reached a finger down to her own cunt and twisted that finger around and around through her own dense bush and into the pleasure hole that it guarded.

The warmth raced through her body now and Karen felt good all over, especially when she saw that someone else had also gotten turned on by the seventeen-year-old's lovely little cunt waving in the air so temptingly.

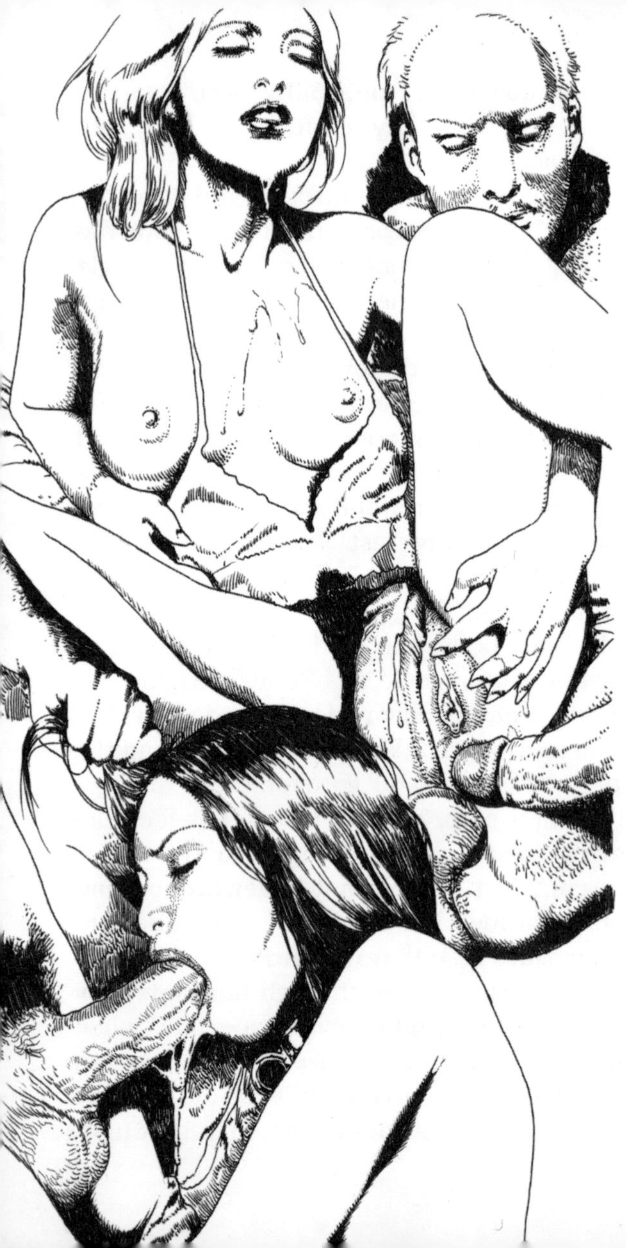

Karen looked away from her own cunt to see who was going to ream Robin. It was her father, Jeffrey, who stood over her drooling, then sinking down to his knees behind his daughter and pushing his rod into her hole. Robin spread her legs and reached down to open her cunt lips slightly, letting Jeffrey's rod slip right in easily. Robin swallowed the cock with her cunt without missing a beat in the going-over she was giving her mother, whose head fell back as she lost control of her body.

Jeffrey moved back and forth slamming his cock into his daughter's hole and with each slam he pushed her harder and harder against her mother's hole. With each push, Diane went further and further into orbit, her head rolled from side to side and her tongue hung out of her open mouth, rolling from side to side as she squirmed in ecstasy.

It was a beautiful scene, albeit a disturbing one and Karen, who was still playing with herself, was getting incredibly turned on, just by watching, although she wasn't sure if the taboo nature of this incestuous grouping had something to do with her arousal. Her cunt hair was soaking wet as her pussy expelled the liquid that was welling up inside her and her slippery fingers had trouble gripping the little bean of her erect clit, but that made the sensation even better as it slipped out of her fingers every time she pinched the little

Orgy Girl ★ 105

pink knob.

Karen rolled over on her stomach and watched the threesome in the corner, intertwined, undulating together, all of them barely in control of what they were doing. Oh, how she yearned for a big stiff cock to be shoved up her slippery split. Karen pulled her hands from her cunt and massaged her entire torso, spreading the pussy juice over her midsection and rubbing it into her tits that were also aching for some action. Karen was so close to ecstasy that her jaw was paralyzed, unable to utter a sound. In the doorway she could see Pete, and she tried to beckon him over to the waterbed. She stared at his stiff cock, but he didn't pay any attention to her. He headed straight for the threesome. His mother's mouth was wide open and it appealed to him. Jeffrey laughed as he slammed his pelvis against his daughter's ass driving his cock home again and saw his son take up a position over his wife's mouth.

Diane opened her eyes and came alive.

"Here, baby, put it in," she whispered between gasps as she opened her mouth even wider, and took Petes cock in her hand and guided it into her mouth. She closed her mouth tight over its red head and rolled it back and forth between her right and left cheeks. But Pete wasn't satisfied, his entire cock ached for action and he wanted to shove all of it down. He grabbed his mother's hair roughly and pulled her head even further back so that it touched the floor. From across the room Karen could see Diane's throat grow tight as her head was bent back in an unnatural position. Pete got down on his knees and pushed his young, stiff cock at his mother's mouth, deeper and deeper. From across the room, Karen could see Diane's throat stretch to accommodate her son's dong. It stretched her tight throat muscles and Karen could almost see the outline of Pete's thing as he plunged it in and out.

Diane could make almost no sound except strangled gurgles as Pete plunged his cock in and out of her mouth and Robin gnawed and sucked at her cunt. Karen was rubbing frantically at her own cunt now, the mad foursome in the corner was turning her green with envy and despite the fact that her cunt was already sopping wet and her body was already covered with her own come she 'couldn't get no satisfaction', as the song went.

When she next looked up, the foursome must have broken up, because there was Pete perched between her spread legs.

"Fuck me, birthday boy!" she urged him.

Pete needed little encouragement. Within seconds his cock buried deep in the bush at her crotch, so deep that she could feel it hammering away against the deepest recesses of her aching slit.

Without even wondering how the hell Pete had gotten on top of her, and without asking, she started moving in unison with him. He leaned on top of her, pressing against her boobs with his hands to get leverage so that he might sink his rod even deeper into her. His hands on her tits felt, oh, so good, and she wanted more and more.

She squirmed around on the waterbed, moving her tits around under his hands so that the nipples, already bright red and erect, slid back and forth under his fingers arousing them even more.

Karen was going to come any minute now and she knew it in every fibre of her body. Her nipples were the first to signal that an orgasm would soon obliterate her mind, but her cunt was beginning to pulsate uncontrollably, gripping and releasing, gripping and releasing Pete's rod and now her arms and legs started twitching. Pete was on the same wavelength as Karen because his ramming motions started to slow down, too. He also was approaching his boiling point and suddenly both bodies merged together in a delightful, simultaneous orgasm. Pete poured the milky contents of his testicles into Karen down the tube of the cock that connected them. Karen arched up to get as much of the potent prick into her as she could. She could feel the waves of her own cum shooting into her, bouncing around the wall of her pleasure cave.

Karen let herself go, yielded to the pent-up passions which had raged in her body as she watched the foursome earlier in its family inter-humping. For one of the first times in her life Karen had gotten immensely horny watching them yet she had been unable to satisfy herself. She didn't know. Perhaps it was the incest thing that bothered her deep down.

It was worth waiting for. As Pete's cock discharged into her, she let out a yelp and then her body went rigid. Her eyes were closed, but she could see a constellation of colours swirling around her head. Pete's hands were still firmly planted on her tits, pinching her nipples between his fingers and this only drove her wilder and wilder. Her back arched and she tossed and turned. Even with Pete on her, the waterbed made it easy for her to move and she practically threw Pete across the room. His cock, completely discharged now, had lost its erection, but that didn't bother Karen in the least. The locked floodgates had been opened wide and she moved up and down, humping some imaginary lover, up and down, around and around, she could feel Pete slide off her now, but even that didn't bother her. She gyrated around and around gradually slowing down as the energy stored up during the massive fucking drained out of her body, leaving her limp and listless on the waterbed.

* * *

Karen didn't know how long she had been lying on the waterbed in a state of total destruction, but eventually she heard a voice calling her.

"Hey, Karen," she heard, "wake up, babe."

She looked up to see that Paul, who had fucked her front and back was jostling her awake.

"You've been lying there for an hour," he laughed, "you'll miss all the fun downstairs."

Karen smiled and extended a hand to Paul who pulled her up and wrapped one of his big meat hooks around her waist. "You're missing Liz doing her thing downstairs," he said leading her to the stairway.

Perched on the stairway, Karen could see that most of the dozen or so guests had formed a circle around a short, but very well-built brunette woman whose hair was cut in a pageboy. Karen remembered her. She was the same Liz who had been at the Witt's orgy a couple of weeks ago, where she had met Mike Huxted. Liz had tried to nail Mike before Karen had, but fortunately Kimberly Witt had intervened. Now she was the centre of attention as she went into a belly dance without anything on.

Karen had to admit that it was very sensual indeed. Liz's body was great and, boy, did she ever know how to use it! She wiggled and squirmed with a great deal of skill, quivering one tit, and then the other, and finally both in harmony. She managed to thrust his hips forward at just the right angle, showing off her pussy with its ringlets of teased, fluffy hair. Her clit poked through the hair seductively and she seemed to have the ability to wiggle it around, too.

Then, in time to the throbbing beat of the loud, funky music, Liz sank into a limbo, spreading her legs wide apart and firmly planting herself in the middle of the circle. She arched her back and let her head fall back. Her nipples were erect and the skin on her torso stretched tight, pressing her tits against her ribcage so the only part that still protruded were the little peaks of her luscious, bullet-like nipples.

She gyrated around and around, brushing her short hair against the floor. Her prominent cunt lips poked through her mound of hair and stood out bright and red for all to see. And still she gyrated her hips and took short steps, forward as if wiggling and squirming her way under an imaginary limbo stick. Liz quickly grabbed a cigar from one of the men in the circle and deftly inserted the burning tube between her cunt lips. Karen could see that every man in the room had a king-sized erection from the performance the little bitch was putting on. Most of the men, without thinking about it, had started toying with their own hard, and semi-hard, cocks even before Liz had jammed the burning cigar into her cunt, but now they were quietly going wild.

Liz was the centre of attraction. She knew it and she was loving every second of it. She clenched and unclenched her cunt lips while still in the limbo position, making it seem like the damned cigar had a life of its own, even making it glow in the subdued light. Every man in the room, with his erection, was envying that cigar crammed into her hot little pussy. The cigar wiggled up and down, and from right to left as Liz twitched the muscles of her cave. Now she started drawing the cigar deeper and deeper into her cunt. But she was careful not to let the burning edge get too close to her fluffy hair-pie.

Now she started pushing the cigar out, laughing and squirming as she surveyed the audience she had so quickly acquired. But this was too much for her. The little act had gotten her excited and Liz just couldn't take it anymore. She let herself fall back on the floor and gripped the big cigar with her hands and started plunging it rapidly in and out of her own hot little cunt.

The excitement built up, and in one quick spasm, Liz came. Liz returned the cigar and wiped the juice away from the little cunt she had just displayed so proudly. The man gratefully took back his loan and with a display of much enjoyment, first licked, then drew upon the soggy end, until he could puff great clouds of blue smoke into the air. A little round of polite applause greeted his act.

"Okay, everybody, let's listen to me now."

That was Jeffrey and he had that mischievous little smile that indicated that he was going to suggest something hot.

"Now the best two lays in the room are Karen and Liz," he started as there was a general murmur of agreement in the room, among both the men who laughed, and the women who smiled as they self-consciously fingered their cunts.

"Hey, listen," Jeffrey started, trying to still the group again. "Let's have a little fight to the finish to see who's the better orgiast. We'll form a circle and whoever pins her opponent first will be crowned the orgiast."

There was another general hum of agreement as the men looked forward to a battle between the two women, both beautiful, but one tall and well put together and the other short and compact. Each with their own distinct style, yet each so juicy and fuckable

Orgy Girl ★ 113

that they could drive any man up a tree.

"Okay, everybody, now these are the rules," Jeffrey called out, "So listen. Both gladiators will have their bodies coated with grease. Both will wear a collar and leash around the neck, and the first one to pin the other for the count of three will win. There will be as many rounds as necessary. And dig this, the winner gets to do anything she wishes to the loser. Anything at all..."

"Okay?" Jeffrey laughed.

The response was unanimous.

"Yeah," someone shouted.

"Dig it."

"Let's go – "

A pair of hands grabbed Karen and before she knew what was happening she found herself spread roughly on the floor and several pairs of hands started assaulting her, smearing her body with a thick layer of perfumed oil. It took a few minutes, but Karen soon got into it. A pair of strong masculine hands cupped one of her tits and vigorously rubbed oil into it, far more persistently than was absolutely necessary. Karen arched her back to push her breasts deeper into the hands that fondled her. She could feel another pair of hands, feminine this time, judging by the long fingernails, rubbing the scented oil through her thick, sweaty bush. The oil felt cool and sweet as it worked its way through Karen's bush and into the gentle folds of her slit and over the pinkish knob of her clit.

Now someone lifted Karen's hair and snapped a leather collar around her neck. The hands felt rough and strong, and the cold of the leather felt good against her oiled body as she wiggled against it. Karen felt the hands clip a short leash to the collar, snapping it shut. Karen couldn't see what was happening to her opponent, but she assumed that Liz was getting the same treatment.

Someone took Karen by the arms and lifted her and pushed her forward. Suddenly Karen found herself in the center of a circle, faced by Liz, also wearing a 'dog collar', her tits glistening and bouncing as she rocked back and forth on her heels.

"Cat fight! Cat fight!" the crowd chanted.

"C'mon, bitches, let's see what you're made of," shouted a woman.

"Well, come on then, bitch, my bitch," Liz hissed, crouching low and stretching her hands out toward Karen, circling her, trying to catch her tall rival from behind.

Karen turned carefully and laced fingers with her opponent, trying to pull her to the ground, but Karen slipped and fell and before she knew what was happening, she felt the breath knocked out of her as Liz leaped on top of her. The straps tangled as the two women rolled on the floor, their greased bodies slipping and sliding around the floor as they struggled with each other.

The crowd yelled its encouragement as the two tumbled madly. Karen felt the long nails of her opponent rake across her body, scratching her all over, and drawing blood from one of her nipples. Strangely, this scratching sent a shiver through Karen's body and she felt her cunt cream. It hurt, but it also felt good. Karen managed to get atop her rival, but couldn't maintain her position because Liz had managed to grab her leash and tug her off balance. She slid off the lithe, well-muscled battler, their tits rubbing each other. Karen was torn by feelings of sensuous desire toward her opponent, but also wanted to beat the shit out of her. Liz struggled atop Karen and dug her oily hands into Karen's thick bush, grabbing a handful and pulling hard. Karen was quickly snapped from her reverie by the sharp pain of this hair-tug. Now she knew that nothing should get in her way. She'd beat the little bitch to within an inch of her life and then fuck her good.

"I wouldn't do that if you know what's good for you," she said.

Liz's only answer was to do it again, only much harder, and this time, Karen let out a yelp when Liz grabbed her pubic hair, but Liz just laughed.

"Can't take it, huh?" she snorted. She

grabbed another handful of hair and pulled yet again. And again Karen screamed, this time louder as she felt the pain shoot from the tips of her cunt hair all through her body. This was a fight to the death and now, she, too, would swing into action.

Karen dug her fingernails into her opponent's body and raked straight down, scoring the skin as she went. Now she could feel Liz's grip on her bush loosening. Karen pulled her hands all the way to Liz's leash and then, grabbing it with her hand, pulled back, tearing Liz off her body and sending her sprawling. Karen jumped up and stood over Liz who was still spread out on the floor, recovering from the spill.

"Come on," Karen hissed. "Get up and take it, bitch."

Liz rolled over and tried to rise, but Karen lashed out with her bare feet and caught her squarely in her gash, knocking the wind out of her.

"Come on, you cheap little whore," Karen yelled, as Liz doubled up with pain. The boot was on the other foot now and Liz wasn't responding, except with gasps for air. Karen jumped on top of her opponent, knocking her to the ground and digging her hands into her bush and pulling hard. Karen rode the little bitch, alternately tugging at Liz's bush, scratching her tits and pummeling her midsection.

Liz's body was covered with bruises, but she still had some fight left in her and now she arched her back spilling Karen onto the floor, but the advantage didn't last long. Liz tried to get up, but before she could Karen caught her off balance and pushed her over, and this time Liz landed on her front. Karen seized her advantage and again mounted Liz, sitting astride her buttocks.

The collar around Karen's neck felt snug and comfortable as she drew long, sweaty breaths. Karen bunched her hand into a fist, but left one knuckle protruding. She brought this down hard, landing a ferocious punch just above Liz's kidney. Liz yelped in pain and arched heir back trying to get loose. Karen didn't yield her advantage for a moment, bringing her fist down hard again in the same spot.

Liz's cry of pain came across loud and clear and now the assembled guests, those who weren't busy rubbing against each other, let out shouts of approval. Karen's body had them all turned on and they were solid in her corner.

Karen bent down over Liz's head and whispered in her ear, "Hold still, you silly bitch, or I'll really cream you."

Liz fell still, stopping her crying and her squirming. Karen relaxed now, sitting astride her opponent. She could feel her oiled skin rubbing against Liz's and it felt good, but Karen was afraid to enjoy it because Liz was the kind of scheming bitch who would take advantage of any opening. But the warm feeling that was spreading through Karen's body was unstoppable, and this combined with Liz's stillness lulled Karen into a sense of false security. As much as she hated the bitch she had conquered, Karen had to admit that she had a good body, the kind any man or even woman could enjoy and that's just what she was doing now. Their oiled bodies felt good against one another and in just a minute or two, Karen could feel her entire body glowing as she continued to rub back and forth against Liz's prone body.

Karen knew that she was running a risk by masturbating now, but the heat of the battle and the spice of the group watching her provided too much raw excitement and she threw her head back and continued rubbing until she felt the warm waves of orgasm washing over her body. The intensity of the orgasm forced Karen to release her grip and it was at that moment that Liz arched her back, flipped Karen neatly onto the ground and bounded up again. Karen's orgasm was rudely brought to a halt as she toppled over.

She felt Liz grab her, but the grab didn't do any good because of the oil all over her body. Karen danced out of the way and whirled around and tried to grab Liz, but her grab attempt also failed. The two women danced around and around, each trying to grab the other but failing as all they managed to grab was slick, oiled skin. Liz was the first one to make contact with the leather strap, grabbing the one tied to Karen's neck. Whoever controlled the strap controlled the match.

Now was the time to end the match and Karen knew that it was now or never. She allowed Liz to grab her strap and pull her close, but then very suddenly, brought her fist forward, sinking it into Liz's soft belly again and again. Liz doubled over in pain. She completely forgot about her grip on Karen's leash, concerned only with the pain that was racking her body. Karen drew her fist back and, once more brought it full into Liz's stomach in a final punch that completely immobilized her. Now she was ready to move in for the kill.

Karen pushed Liz over. It didn't take much energy since the winded Liz was as helpless as a kitten. Karen straddled Liz. This time not getting turned on as their cunts came into contact. Nothing would divert Karen from her final victory now and Karen grabbed the collar around Liz's neck and twisted it. Liz was moaning in agony, and now the new pressure was too much for her. The collar cut viciously into her neck and now her sobs were broken and irregular. She could barely squeeze out another sound as the collar tightened around her windpipe cutting off her air supply.

"Beg for mercy you two-bit whore," Karen hissed at her downed opponent.

"Please, please let go," Liz begged. "Let go."

"Plead for mercy, you bitch," Karen laughed.

"Oh, please, Mercy, mercy," Liz gasped.

"Again, you bitch," Karen murmured, "again." This time Karen twisted the collar even more almost entirely cutting off Liz's ability to breathe. Liz's legs thrashed about aimlessly. She was unable to control them and unable to do anything about the death grip Karen had on her.

"Oh, please, let go," Liz whispered. "You win, you win. I'll do anything, anything you want."

Those were the words Karen wanted to hear.

She had a special punishment in mind for this little bitch and now she would get to administer it. Karen released her grip and let the collar untwist. Liz took a deep breath and everyone in the room applauded as Karen bounded up and held her hands over her head as a champion should.

"Well, Karen, what would you like to do?" Jeffrey asked.

"Give me that, I'm going to hump that little baby right up her ass," Karen grinned, pointing at the dildo.

She strapped the dildo on, inserting one end into her own twat so she could feel it as she hammered into Liz's ass.

Liz could see what was coming and she tried to squirm away, but a couple of men grabbed her and laid her over the arm of a couch, holding her down and exposing her rich, plump ass.

"She's all yours, Karen," Jeffrey smiled.

Karen approached her victim and without any attempt to ease her entry humped forward ramming the dildo into Liz's ass. Liz let out a scream, but the scream felt good to Karen's ears. The excitement was too much for Karen who felt the dildo ramming her own cunt. Karen's clit tingled deliciously as the dildo rubbed against it. The dildo moved roughly in and out of Liz's ass and she continued to scream and beg for mercy, but Karen no longer had any for the little bitch who had tried to take advantage of her.

In and out, in and out, the dildo tunneled a wide, gaping hole in Liz's ass as it gently tickled Karen's cunt. It was as it should be, the winner fucking the hell out of the loser.

The waves of warm, sensuous vibrations raced through Karen's body. The group cheered her on as they watched her humping backward and forward, her tits jumping about madly.

This time Karen had nothing to fear as her body grew hotter and hotter. She completely shut out of her mind Liz's cries of pain as the dry dildo plunged in and out of her ass. Karen couldn't care less. Spurts of tainted cum exploded from Liz's aching asshole, who had obviously had plenty of anal sex that evening, but Karen didn't care. She was an inch short of orgasm and she made one more, deep forward plunge. Liz's scream split the air as the dildo went further into her ass than before, but Karen didn't care, her orgasm was starting.

"Ahhhhh!" she cried as her body shook and jittered as the dildo slithered out of her opponent's exhausted body, followed by an obscene gush of sperm that had been deposited by several of her lovers that night. Liz's humiliation was complete.

Chapter 6

Karen's body was sore all over. Her asshole had been thoroughly cornholed, her cunt had been reamed sore and her throat had been scraped and banged. Her tits were aching from the sucking and biting she'd gotten, but Karen loved it. In fact, her body never felt good unless it had been brutally overused and although the humping she'd done before the wrestling match with Liz was nothing to sneeze at, what happened afterward was even better.

Liz had been left lying in a corner to nurse her wounds and two of the men had picked Karen up and carried her to the bar and threw her atop it. Someone had fashioned a wreath of plastic flowers and someone else jammed it down over Karen's head. The flowers felt scratchy, but Karen continued to wear them, and after a couple of rounds of drinks, Karen fulfilled one of her greatest fantasies. She took on every, man and woman in the room, two and three at a time.

The evening faded into a blur for Karen but she recalled one man shoving his cock up her asshole while another chewed her cunt, and others grabbed at her tits. Male and female hands together pawed her. Suddenly she felt a pair of hands prying her lips apart and before she knew it someone shoved his rod into her mouth. Karen threw her head back and swallowed it eagerly. It wasn't very big but it went down easily and soon she could feel come pouring down her throat and over her lips and dripping down her chest, where

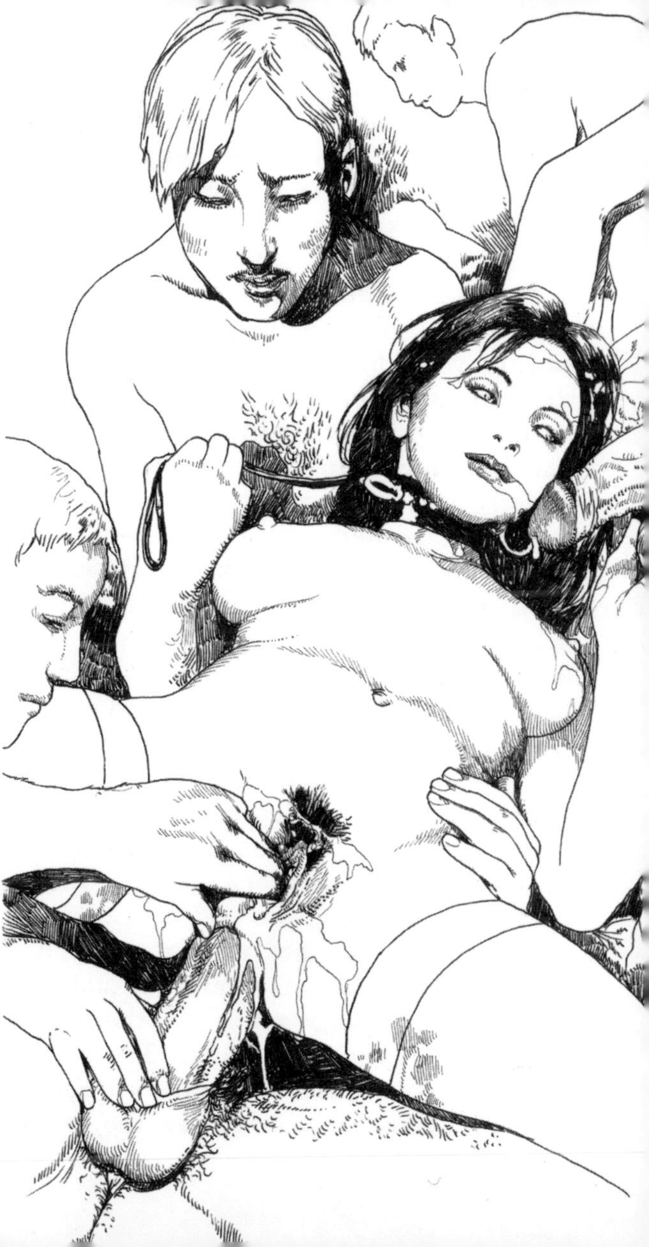

it mingled with the sweat and oil and where the groping hands of the group massaged it vigorously into every pore of her skin.

She was aware of a constantly changing cavalcade of cocks, rods, cunts, slits, tools and hands, hands, hands, tearing at her body and using her. Later, she couldn't really remember who had done what, but she knew exactly what had been done to her from the various different parts of her body that ached so deliciously. And there was one thing that Karen did remember because it was an entirely new experience for her.

One of the men pulled the others off and pushed Karen down to her knees. He stepped back and let loose a long stream of piss, hosing Karen's hot body down with his warm liquid. It felt hot and it felt good as it splashed her nipples and over her tits and trickled down her body. Soon another stream joined the rust and then another and another. Now Karen was being doused by an ocean of hot piss and it felt even better. Karen cupped her hands and caught some of it, playfully flinging it back at her attackers and at the women who watched. Another woman dropped to the floor beside Karen, joining her under the barrage of piss, flinging it at the others as she caught it in her cupped hands. The hot piss washed the sweet oil and come off Karen's body and Karen wondered how the barrage of urine could keep coming for so long, but somehow it did. Some of the women kept up the flow by half squatting and, thrusting their pelvises forward, gushing a stream of pee into their faces at close quarters.

And when they had emptied their bladders they reached for two seltzer bottles behind the bar, squirting it at the two women who wallowed in the cold fluid which was a welcome change from the hot streams of the last few minutes.

Karen was wet from head to toe and after that she could remember only snatches of the rest of the evening. She'd humped Jeffrey and Pete again, and had had a very long sensuous session with Robin and had finally ended up with Meredith, a short squat fireplug of a man who looked totally sexless, but could nevertheless hump the brains out of any poor working girl. Meredith had dragged Karen off to a corner and taken her on a trip around the world, coming to rest in her asshole, which had opened nice and wide by now and was eager to accept any tool, then in her cunt, which was scraped sore but still ready for action and climaxing in her mouth by sending torrents of come deep into her stomach. Karen hadn't eaten all night, but she really didn't need to with all that sweet come she was devouring.

Karen felt a hand gently squeezing her

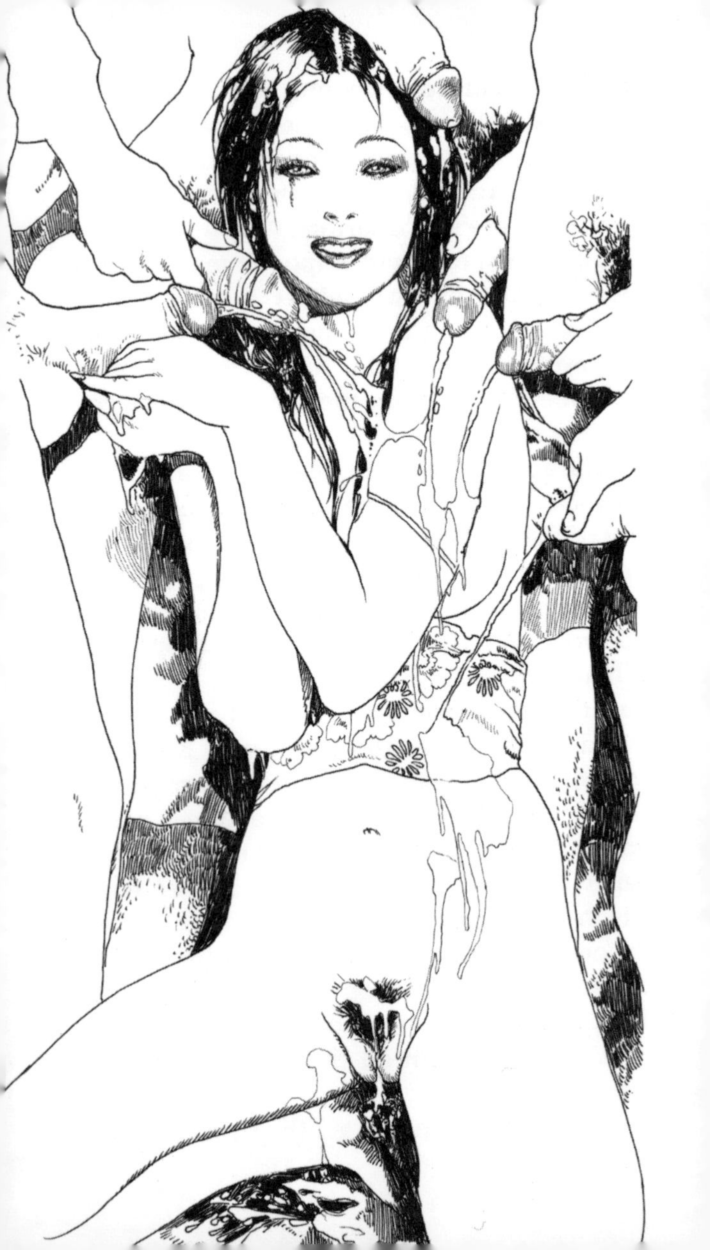

tits and she started waking up, realizing now that she was in the back seat of a limousine. Karen opened one eye and surveyed the surroundings. She was completely nude, with a large cloak draped around her body. The screen between driver and passenger compartments was closed and she was aware that Meredith was squeezing her tits gently.

"Wake up, baby, we're almost there," he whispered.

"Where?" Karen replied, yawning as she squeezed that one word out.

"The airport," he laughed. "We're going off to the Virgin Islands, my love, to visit my little shack on the beach."

"That's nice," Karen yawned, looking around the little passenger compartment. Now her eyes fell on Liz who was sitting on the jump seat, her head bent low over Meredith's crotch giving him a blow-job. Meredith's cock was obviously still as good as ever despite the humping of the night before because it was as big and stiff as it ever was, and it was much too large for Liz to swallow.

"What's *she* doing here?" Karen snarled at Meredith.

"Don't worry, she's promised to behave herself I'm sure you two can learn to get along, right?" Meredith asked Liz.

Without missing a beat of her blow-job, Liz nodded her head and Meredith shivered as the sensations of the wiggle spread through his rod and up into his body.

"I couldn't find your clothes when we left," he said to Karen, "so I just wrapped you in your cloak. We'll get you some new ones once we land in the Virgins."

The limousine rolled through the airport gates and into the private hanger where Meredith kept his Lear jet. Karen hopped from the car and hurried into the plane, barefoot and bare-assed. The inside of the plane was air conditioned and a little chilly. Liz, who followed Karen into the plane pointed to the rear compartment.

"It'll be warmer in there," she said as she took Karen's hand and led her in.

"Make yourselves comfortable, we'll take off in about ten minutes," Meredith shouted to the girls and then turned to talk with the attendant and his co-pilot. He was going to pilot this flight himself.

The rear compartment was outfitted with a twin-bed-sized cot and Karen, still sleepy, lay down on it and drew the cloak around her. She was still cold and shivered in the cool cabin. Liz kicked her shoes off and lay down beside Karen, squirming under the cover and offering her body to Karen to help her keep warm.

Liz, who was still fully dressed, had a hot little body and Karen appreciated the gesture. She curled up and pressed her body beside Liz's, rubbing their cheeks together. Karen was beginning to warm up now, and she leaned over and kissed Liz on the cheek. Liz stirred slightly and turned her head, offering her lips to Karen.

Karen was willing to bury the hatchet and she accepted Liz's lips, returning the kiss. Their lips almost came glued together. Karen's were cold and Liz's were burning hot. Before Karen knew what happened, Liz had rolled over on her and had poked her tongue deep into Karen's mouth. Her tongue rolling around in Karen's mouth felt good and Karen felt herself becoming aroused again. Karen reached for Liz's blouse and started undoing the buttons. Liz shifted her body to make Karen's task easier. Only three of the buttons had been fastened and it took barely a minute until Liz's healthy tits were hanging loose, brushing over Karen's own, larger tits.

Liz's tits showed the signs of last night's battle, but they felt good and hot as they brushed against Karen's. Liz rolled over on her back and slipped her micro-skirt down her hips, letting it fall to the floor. Karen's, slow return to consciousness had given her an overpowering urge to eat Liz's sweet pussy and now, still huddled under the cloak which covered them both, she squirmed down toward the foot of the bed so she could sink her teeth into Liz's furry little gash. Last night she had kicked and scratched it as viciously as she could and now, just a few hours later, she was barely able to control herself as she sniffed the sweet cunt and licked the little pink nub above it and the wrinkled, fleshy lips which shielded it. Liz who had fought so hard and so dirty the night before knew that this morning things were different. She had been vanquished and beaten, but now she was being loved.

Liz spread her legs and arched her back offering her hungry little cunt up to Karen who was anxious to accept it. Karen started slowly licking Liz's cunt from top to bottom and from bottom to top in long, slow, smooth motions, curling her tongue through the cunt hair and teasing Liz's cunt lips to get her warmed up for the final assault. Little beads of moisture started dripping from Liz's cunt and hanging from the edges of her cunt lips. The drops of pussy juices were either absorbed by the furry cunt hair or were licked away by Karen who was savouring every drop of Liz's sticky-sweet pussy juice.

Liz was having trouble controlling herself and now she started writhing against the rug, feeling her smooth skin stimulated up by the slightly rough fabric. Liz desperately wanted to feel Karen's tongue take the plunge deep into her body, but Karen was playing the tease now and she knew that she had Liz on the ropes; Karen was enjoying slow process of torturing Liz. Karen moved her tongue up and down and back and forth across Liz's pert little pudendal mound, lingering at the floppy pink inner lips that were enlarged now by the flow of blood that rushed down to Liz's arousal point.

Karen was enjoying herself too damned much to let Liz off the hook completely and she continued the slow motion. Liz was too hot and she couldn't take any more. She arched her hips higher and higher, as if trying to suck Karen's tongue into her cunt, but it was to no avail. Karen had Liz and she wasn't letting go. But at last the pressure became too much. The juice continued to flow from Liz's cunt and to lick it faster, Karen could not resist sticking her tongue deep into Liz's warm, wet, fragrant hole and as she did, Liz arched her back almost a foot off the bed, rising up to swallow Karen's tongue.

The result was as if an aerial shell had burst inside the girl's head. Liz started seeing stars and flashes of light as her orgasm raced through her body, short-circuiting her entire nervous system. Liz's body was locked into the arched position as she squeezed out a long, soft shriek. Karen kept her tongue inside Liz's juddering body because the juice was flowing so copiously now. But at last – it seemed like it had gone on for hours – Liz's orgasm ended and she collapsed in a bundle, rolling up almost into a ball in a corner of the mattress.

Karen had pulled her tongue back and fallen on the other side of the bed, and now she was aware of the movement of the plane. She looked out the window and could see that the plane was in the air, but she could still see the runway far below. In mutual rapture, as they rocked and rolled on the bed, she and Liz had missed the takeoff.

Karen smiled. How very considerate of Meredith not to have disturbed their humping session with tiresome announcements about seat belts and so on. It had been a nice smooth takeoff for Meredith piloting the plane and, come to think of it, for Karen piloting Liz, who was only now regaining her composure.

Liz reached out to Karen and then the naked girls embraced. Their tits rubbed against each other and warmth spread through both bodies.

"It's been a long time since I had it that good," Liz whispered to Karen, hugging her.

"Me too, baby," Karen replied, continuing the hug and rubbing her tits back and forth across Liz's.

"Let's lie down and rest," Liz urged Karen. "It'll be a long flight and there'll be a lot for us to do once we land."

"You've done this before?" Karen asked.

"Uh-huh," Liz nodded, "and, I can tell you hon, it's a real blast."

"Tell me about it now!" Karen implored.

"No, you'll see for yourself. It's always better that way – more of a surprise," Liz smiled. "Relax, it's fun."

"Well, then, tell me about yourself," Karen asked. "I know nothing about you. Tell me about the first time. Tell me about how you lost your cherry."

Karen lay back and held her arm out for Liz to lie down and curl up next to her.

"Okay," Liz said, a twinkle in her eye, as she reclined and thought about her long-lost cherry.

* * *

"When I lost my cherry, I lost it with a real bang. I was a cheerleader and the football team was playing for the state-wide championship. Until that day I had been a pretty little virgin, even my boyfriend had never gotten beyond my tits. Anyway, the team was losing at half time so we decided to goose them a little. We promised them us if they won," Liz laughed.

"Hell, for your body, I'd go out there and knock 'em dead," Karen laughed.

"Anyway, Coach went along with it and we

didn't even know how to have an orgy. But the team won and after we got back home, Coach arranged for us to have a barbecue behind the school stadium," Liz continued.

"He knew what was going to happen and he didn't care because we won the championship. Anyway, we all got there and nobody knew what to do except Helena. She was the shortest one of the cheerleaders but she had the biggest knockers, and rumour had it that she would hump anyone.

Anyway, she had already slept with most of the team and she showed us how to do it. She shucked off her clothing one piece at a time. Most of the guys were drunk and they were cheering like mad. Shit, it was an awful scene. I mean, there we were, a dozen virgins scared out of our pants. Most of us had tiny little boobies, and almost bare little slits, and there she was with a pair that hung like watermelons and her big hairy gash.

The guys started getting undressed, and they were practically tripping over their hard-ons. Anyway, a couple of guys made it with her and then the action really started. We were dancing around all nude and it started raining and we wallowed in the mud – humping and fucking. I don't know where I learned to do it all but it seemed so natural that I just kept doing it. I must have had five or six guys that night and one or two of the girls, including Helena."

Liz looked down at Karen who had become increasingly sleepy and who had just about dozed off as she had finished her little tale. Liz lay back and thought more about that magical evening that was at first so frightening, but turned out so beautiful. There was, of course, more to tell than she had told, and now she lay back and thought back to those innocent sixteen-year-old days.

Yes, Helena had been the first one to wave her hairy gash at the boys, but most of them had wanted Liz and the first to get her was José, a swarthy Latino and good-looking leader of the team. Both were still dressed when he wrapped his arm around her and with his other hand reached up her skirt. Liz made no effort to resist. She knew she was going to get laid that night and she was glad that José picked her out.

His strong hand plucked at her panties and pulled them down. Liz could feel the chill air on her almost-naked pussy. José laced his fingers over her cunt lips and plucked them slightly. Liz felt a feeling like she'd never known before. Her whole body started singing and she had barely been touched.

José pulled his hands away and started undressing. Liz followed suit, stripping her skirt and sweater off without any modesty, but then pausing, afraid to pull her bra and panties all the way off since it seemed such a complete and irretrievable step to take – to show herself naked. One look at Helena, her legs waving in the air and some football player riding her, and another look as José skinned his shorts off convinced her. She'd barely finished stripping when José grabbed her in his arms and started smothering her with kisses. She felt his cool skin and his erect organ pressing against her and she let her body just hang in José's arms.

José held her against his body, kissing her and kneading her ass as he held her. So this was paradise, Liz thought as she felt José scoop her up in his arms and carry her towards a quiet, grassy corner where he laid her down gently.

"I've never done this before," Liz whispered to her ardent young lover.

"Don't worry. I have and I'll take care of you," he smiled, kissing her full on the lips and working his way down her body, kissing each of her young tits, sucking on the small, budding, erect nipples and tenderly licking her midriff. Liz had practically no hair shielding her cunt and José licked over the exposed lips, watching them grow red as they filled with blood.

Liz was getting excited. She'd never felt the kind of blush that spread through her body. She'd never even masturbated before and now her body was super-heated with passion. She didn't quite know why, but she spread her legs wide. She didn't know what was happening because her eyes were shut tight and her hands dug deep into the grass around her. She clenched and unclenched her hands, digging up the grass and she wiggled her hips back and forth under the attack of José's tongue, which brushed back and forth over and around her ever-reddening cunt lips. Liz was uttering short moans and grunts as José flicked his tongue in and out of her cunt. Suddenly Liz felt her whole body catch fire, every fiber of her skin and bone was flaming and she wanted to scream, scream, scream, but she found her jaws locked in the wide open position unable to utter a sound. She didn't know it yet, but she'd just had her first orgasm. And there were more to come.

Very gently, José lay his body atop Liz's. It felt nice and cool against her burning skin and still reacting automatically. Liz raised her legs and locked them around José's waist. She could feel his stiff rod pressing against her cunt lips and she could feel him pressing down and his swollen glans about an inch inside of her was stopped by the thin membrane of her hymen that guarded the tunnel of her vagina and, ultimately, her very womb.

Suddenly, it was all over. José shoved forwards and, in one blinding flash of pain,

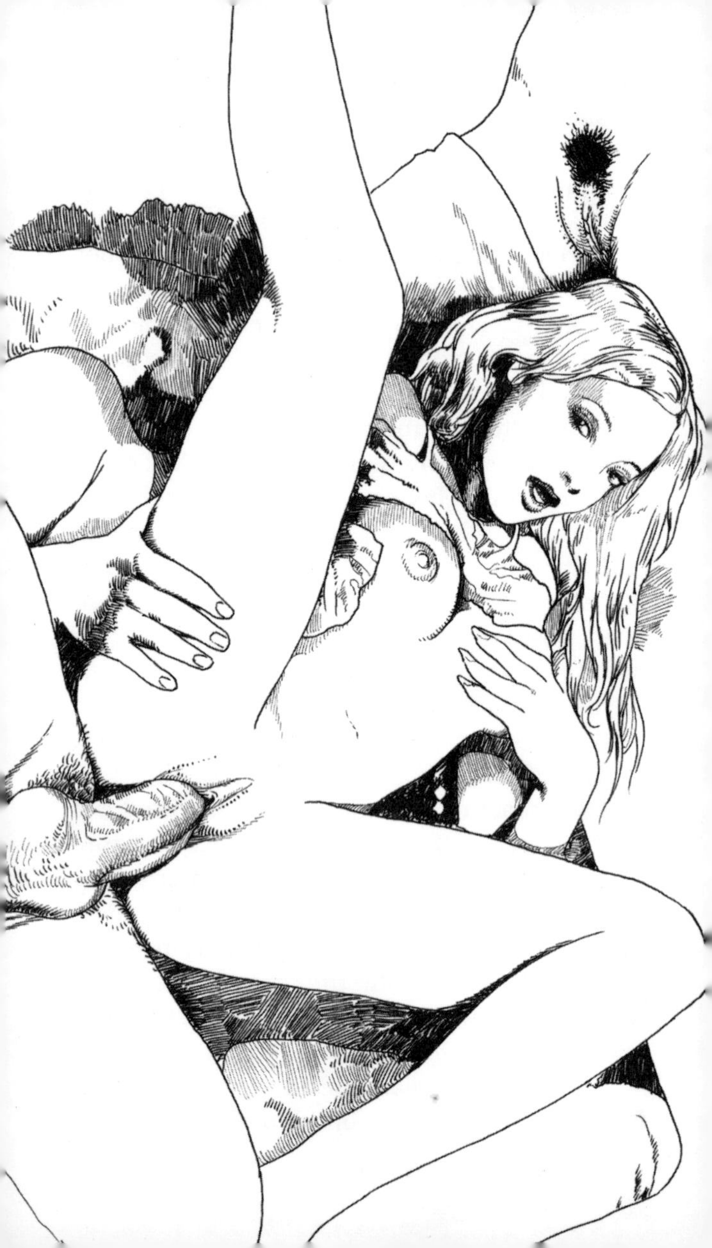

the tender little skin was ruptured and José's cock slipped all the way into her tight hole. The pain was quickly replaced by pleasure as José started thrusting his cock in and out, in and out, against the constricting, rubbery walls of her twat.

For a second time, Liz felt her body catch fire and felt the blood pound through every vein in her body. Orgasm number two, and still she wasn't sure of just what had happened except that it was the best thing that had ever happened to her, even surpassing the orgasm of a few moments before.

And that best thing happened to her again and again that night as she tried the other championship team members. Her young cunt, which had done nothing for the previous years of her life was filled to capacity with her own pussy juice and the sperm of the others. Liz was the most popular member of the cheerleading team and after that first session with José one of the most willing. She had to learn exactly what that hot, fiery feeling that started in her cunt and spread through the rest of her body was.

She tried big cocks and little ones, thick ones and thin ones and each of them went sliding into her warm little hole and pounded her without mercy, which was just what she wanted. Soon her rapidly learning little twat would grow as hairy as Helena's, and Helena, who until that night had been the most popular girl in school, and the easiest lay, found herself displaced by the little vixen with lots to learn and all the enthusiasm to learn it.

* * *

Liz's dreams were interrupted now by the bump-bump of the small jet landing. Karen was just waking up now also, and Liz could see that although both were asleep, each in their own dream world, they had both been dreaming of the same thing. Karen's mouth had fallen open and she had drooled in her sleep down her own chest and onto Liz's, who, on the other hand, had found her own index finger buried deep in her own slippery-wet cunt.

"Well, we're here," Meredith smiled, poking his head out of the cockpit.

Karen reached for the cloak in which she'd been wrapped, but Liz interrupted her.

"You won't need that here," she laughed. "We're right on the beach near the house. There's no one around but the servants and they're used to it."

"Well, that's nice, I could use a bit of catching up on my tan," Karen smiled, wiping her own tits with a bit of the cloak and reaching to do the same for Liz.

"Okay, girls, hop out after me and let's

head for a nice, cool drink at the house," Meredith said, opening the door to the plane and descending the steps.

Liz bowed low to Karen and motioned her to the door.

"After you, Queen Bitch!" she laughed merrily.

"Thank you, love," Karen smiled at her former rival, putting her arm around her and squeezing gently, remembering just how fine Liz's body had felt and being glad of the reminder.

Liz felt a warm glow from Karen's squeeze and put her own arm around Karen's back allowing it to fall over Karen's ass, gently running one of her fingertips along the crack of her smooth, shapely posterior.

Both of them stepped nude out of the small jet and blinked fiercely as the bright sunshine flooded across their bodies and they descended onto the hot tarmac of the landing strip by the long, sandy beach. The jet had taxied to a halt not a hundred yards from the superb beach house itself. Some 'shack', thought Karen.

Chapter 7

The sun beat down fiercely and after the air conditioned chill of the Lear's cabin, the burning rays of the sun hitting their skin warmed them immediately. Meredith had already started toward the house that was set among a dense clump of gently swaying palm trees. He had pulled his shirt off and was undoing his pants and kicking his shoes off, letting them fall as he walked. From the house a black youngster, perhaps fifteen years old, ran toward Meredith.

"Valston, please fetch the suitcases off the plane," Meredith commanded, swatting the youngster on his backside as he laughed and ran to do as he was bid.

He was tall and strong for his age as he stooped to pick up Meredith's scattered clothing on his way to the beached jet. He caught sight of the two white women, nude and walking arm in arm toward the house. He waved cheerily and didn't seem at all surprised.

"That's Valston," Liz said to Karen. "He's the general houseboy and takes care of the odds and ends around here, even your end, if you'd like."

"That's nice," Karen said surveying the youngster who struggled to pry one of the suitcases out of the plane. He also seemed to be struggling with a very obvious erection that was pushing against the tattered shorts he was wearing.

"Don't stare so hard, baby," Liz teased Karen, giving her buttocks another gentle squeeze. "His mother Thelma is the cook and housekeeper. She's a favourite with Meredith. He treats her like a queen."

The two continued to the house, looking up at the lush tropical growth that started so suddenly where the beach ended. The house itself was massive, with a large basement, a dining-living area that took up the whole first floor and a half-dozen bedrooms, each with its own full bath upstairs.

Karen stared with open eyes at the expensive furniture and paintings, while Liz, who had seen it all before, watched Karen with some amusement.

"Relax, baby," she laughed. "You'll get used to all this splendour before long."

"Hello, ladies," a rich, deep, contralto voice cut in from the background. Karen whirled to see who it was. "I'm Thelma. Master told me to show you to your rooms."

Karen surveyed the woman who stepped out of the doorway. She was tall, almost as tall as Karen and had a large figure. Big boobs drooping forward, a thick, but firm waist and large ample hips that suggested childbirth and a lifetime of hard work. Her hair was drawn back in a bun and her skin was as black as any Karen had ever seen. Her body was draped in a thin cotton frock with a row of buttons down the center. Half the buttons were open, allowing her enormous cleavage to show and Karen could see that Thelma didn't believe in bras and had large prominent nipples the size of her thumb tips jutting straight out. Thelma didn't believe in panties either, because as Karen lowered her eyes she could see that Thelma's skin was pressed flush against the frock in a couple of places where sweat had plastered it to her body. A couple of the kinky hairs from her gash had somehow pushed through the flimsy cotton frock that ended about a foot or so above her knee.

"This way, Ladies," she said, charming them both with her strong Caribbean lilt, leading the two upstairs.

"That's Master's room," she said, pointing to the end of the hallway. Miss Liz is in this room and Miss Karen is here. If you want anything I'll be downstairs."

Thelma turned and plodded down the stairs. Meredith had the corner bedroom. Karen had been placed next to him and Liz next to Karen. Not a bad arrangement, Karen thought to herself.

"Well, kiddo," Liz said. "I don't know about you, but I could use a good, hot bath. I'll see you later." Liz ran her fingertips across Karen's ass, gave it a friendly slap and slithered into her room.

"Yeah," Karen echoed. "See you later."

Karen walked into her room and surveyed it. There was a big double bed – naturally, Karen smiled to herself – a couple of chairs and the usual bedroom furniture as well as some nice colourful pictures on the wall, obviously by a local artist. On the table by the window there was a tray loaded with exotic fruits, delicate bread rolls, butter and jam and a huge steaming pot of coffee. Heaven! After devouring most of the breakfast tray's contents and downing several cups of coffee, Karen thought that what she needed most next was a bath.

The bathroom was large and had an extra large-sized tub. Karen reached over and turned the hot water on letting it splash into the tub. Without waiting for it to fill she stepped into it and lay down flat, slithering over to the end of than tub which had the faucet and lifting her legs in a V so her slit would be under the running water. She wiggled and squirmed to get the right position so that the water would gush over and into her gash pounding away at her clit. Karen reached over and pulled the plug out of the tub. She didn't want the tub filling with water. She just wanted to lie flat against its cool surface so that her cunt could get the pounding it was aching for. She spread her legs farther and farther apart and opened her cunt lips with her fingers, parting her hair and laying the pink inner lips open and bare to the hot gushing water.

Karen's cunt filled with the hot water in a matter of seconds, but she kept her lips spread wide and the water pounded into them and the water that was already in her cunt spurted up and out in little streams. Her pink clit turned redder and redder under the force of the water and Karen felt a strange heat spreading through her body that had nothing to do with the hot water.

Her fingers grew numb and her cunt lips slipped from her fingers, closing over the pool of water trapped in her cave. The water pounded against her closed lips now and splashed and splattered all over the tub bouncing across her tits and spilling over her nipples, which also ached for action. Karen was still alive, but she had lost control of her body. She was conscious but unable to do anything but feel the burning pounding that was pushing her inexorably to orgasm.

Karen was too freaked-out to recognize what was happening, but suddenly she was no longer under the pounding hot faucet. The first flash of orgasm had streaked through her body and she'd twisted into a series of contortions. She flopped over on her belly and then on her side. Her legs thrashed about splashing water all over the tub, all over her and all over the bathroom's tiled floor.

The hot water splashing about felt good wetting Karen's body all over as she jigged about against the cool enamel of the bathtub. Karen tried desperately to jam her fingers into her hole, but her body had taken on a life of its own and it was having its own orgasm, wildly gyrating under the stream of hot water.

It seemed like an hour later that Karen came, too, somehow dragged herself to the tub's drain, put the plug back in so the tub could fill with water and then collapsed under the strain of her orgasm as the tub filled with water and floated her body back to reality.

Karen finally opened her eyes and surveyed the room. It was a mess. There was water splattered all over the white-tiled room, the toilet seat and the mirror over the sink were all wet. Karen had taken a lovely comfortable bathroom and destroyed it with one single orgasm. Karen fingered her tits and looked around the room, laughing at the mess she'd made, but relieved that she'd caused no permanent damage.

She wasn't sure, but she thought she heard scratching sound. Karen turned toward the open door and there stood Valston, tentative and bashful. Karen reacted without thinking, letting out a loud gasp and trying to cover herself. But then she burst out laughing as Valston quickly stepped behind the door in embarrassment. She wasn't used to flashing her muff at fifteen-year-olds and had completely forgotten that Valston had already gotten a thorough view of her, tits, ass, cunt and all.

"Come on back, Valston," Karen called out. "I'm sorry, it's just that you startled me. Come here!"

Timidly the young man peered around the door and then entered the bathroom, stepping barefoot in one of the puddles.

"It's okay, Valston," Karen said when she saw the puzzled look on his face. "I splashed the water and made the mess."

"I'll mop it up later," Valston said smiling.

"Don't ... Thank you," Karen said, looking over the young man. If he was only fifteen, she thought to herself, he had one hell of a body, and that body came equipped with a nice cock as she could plainly see by the bulge in his shorts.

"Miss Liz say Miss Karen maybe like a massage. It is my specialty, ma'am!" said the boy proudly.

"Sure," Karen said sensing an opening.

"Shall I get out of the tub?"

"No, Miss Karen," Valston replied stepping closer. "Stay in the tub, I'll climb in, tub's big enough for the two of us."

"Be my guest," Karen smiled as Valston started climbing into the tub.

"But take those shorts off, you'll only get them wet in here," she continued.

"Sure thing, Miss Karen," Valston smiled. "Wouldn't do to get my shorts wet."

He slipped gracefully out of them, sliding them down his hips, drawing one leg up and pulling it off and then drawing the other leg through the shorts. He flipped them through the open door and onto the dry rug in the next room. Karen surveyed her young masseur. His limbs were strong and well formed, but although he was on the skinny side, his body was equipped with plenty of tough, stringy muscles. There was a fuzz of kinky hair around his generous cock, which was now beginning to stir amid that fuzz and come to life. Even in its non-erect state it was large.

Karen spread her legs so that each touched one wall of the tub. She didn't feel like talking any more, so she just gestured to the area between her legs. Valston had been here before and knew how to pick up a hint. He stepped nimbly over the wall of the tub and over Karen's legs and fell to his knees in the water between her legs. He stared at the rich, hairy muff that beckoned him, and at the large tits that anticipated his strong hands kneading them.

He stretched his arms wide and flexed his muscles and leaned down to Karen. Planting one hand on each of her open thighs he dug his strong fingers in, kneading her flesh and stretching it over her bones.

Valston had strong hands and Karen felt shivers running through her body as the black houseboy dug into her flesh and moved his hands up and down her thighs from her knees to her hips, kneading and pressing and waking up long-lost nerves. Yes, Karen thought to herself, Valston had been here before and he knew exactly how to work his way up to the precise moment when he would bring Karen to the brink of total bliss.

He slid his hands up her hips and massaged her belly now, pressing hard and deep into Karen's muscular, well-developed midriff. He worked in expanding circles around Karen's bellybutton, alternately pressing with his fingertips and then with his knuckles. At first Karen had been apprehensive about the young man, but now she abandoned herself completely to his strong manipulative hands.

Now Valston concentrated on Karen's ribs, running his knuckles over them, back and forth, digging between them and pushing them apart. The pain of reawakening raced through her body from head to toe and back again. Valston knew his work and proceeded carefully. He gripped Karen's right tit between both his hands and pressed it together into a roll. Then he rolled it back and forth between both his hands, carefully pinching the nipple and releasing it, pinching it and releasing it, continuing to roll and squeeze it. It was a feeling that Karen had never experienced before. Her mouth fell open and she could feel the saliva dripping down her chin, but she didn't have the strength to snap her jaws closed.

Valston reached over to the other tit and gave it the same treatment. Karen felt her body growing hotter and hotter. Valston pressed his knee against her patch and Karen rubbed her hips up and down feeling his smooth, silky black knee against her cunt through her bush of hair. Her own hair was turning her on now and Karen was completely surrendering to the ministrations of the fifteen-year-old houseboy.

Valston continued rolling one tit between both his hands but now he bent his head down and sucked the other nipple between his teeth nipping and biting it gently around and around in circles. Karen felt her entire body short-circuiting itself Valston was assaulting every one of her pleasure spots. Karen ached to feel his cock inside of her, but he was stronger than she and he hadn't finished his massage yet. She could feel his heavy cock leaning against her belly as he switched tits, now rolling the left one while nipping at the right one with his teeth.

He was bringing her along very slowly to a first orgasm, working slowly to both bring it on and to delay it, dragging her to the brink of total annihilation and then pulling her back.

"Oh, please, let me come, let me," Karen pleaded.

"Oh, no, Miss Karen, hold back, hold back a little," Valston whispered, "be *much* better if you hold back!"

"No, now, I want my orgasm *now!*" Karen begged, squirming, pushing her pelvis up as if she could have her orgasm by reaching out for it and grabbing it. But Valston kept her balanced on the edge, almost feeling herself coming, yet not quite coming as he continued rolling one tit and sucking on the other and pushing his knee against her patch.

Valston pulled back for a moment and lifted Karen's legs so that her thatch became a target point for his stiff cock. Very gently, with thumb and index finger Valston spread her cunt lips. Karen knew what was coming and drew a deep breath in expectation. In a moment Valston's rod would plunge through her bush, past her reddened cunt lips and deep into her hole. Karen knew that this would indeed be the moment of total wipeout orgasm. Valston moved back on his knees, leaned forward with his hands on Karen's tits and allowing himself to fall forward. His cock moved in a perfect arc and scored a perfect hit moving gracefully through Karen's wet bush of black cunt hair, pushing smoothly past her wet cunt lips, moistened by the anticipation and foreplay and slid smoothly into the pink tunnel that started at her cunt lips and had its nerve endings deep in the back of Karen's skull.

For Karen, who squinted her eyes shut the minute she felt Valston fall forward, the whole scene took place in slow motion. She felt her cunt hair tickle as his cock moved through them. It felt like it lasted for five minutes despite the fact that his cock sliced through her bush in just instants. Karen then felt her hot red cunt lips pried apart as though someone had jammed a hydraulic jack between those lips and turned it on full. Her labia were shoved wide apart, stretching the skin like it had never before been stretched, further than she would have thought possible. She imagined her cave being torn to shreds by the massive weapon being violently shoved up her well-greased cunt tunnel. Karen had begged and pleaded and now she felt the chain reaction start. The sensation spread like wildfire from the vortex of her twat and spread in ever-widening circles throughout her entire body, encompassing her tits, her ass and her entire being.

But before the orgasm could spread to every inch of her body, Valston started rocking back and forth on her body plunging his enormous young tool in and out, slamming his flat, hard black belly against her well-muscled white belly. His cock sank deep into her, tearing away at her walls and slamming into the back wall. Karen could barely keep breathing under the assault and didn't really care whether she did or not. She arched her back, bringing her belly up to meet his. The slap was deafening as the two bodies met in hard contact, but the effect of the slapping motion poured even more fuel onto the flames of desire that burned inside Karen. Valston's rod slammed away at every nerve ending sending shudders racing through her entire body.

Each successive orgasm raced and overtook the proceeding one like ripples on a lake. One after another, with short grunts and gasps, Karen's voice signalled her pain/pleasure and the sound echoed and bounced around the tiled walls of the bathroom. At last her body could not take any more and she felt herself slowing down, but then she felt a strange pulsating motion in Valston's prick. She felt him shooting his load deep into her. Her cunt swung into action, twitching and wiggling, wringing his tool as best she could. She knew that the streams of hot come shooting deep inside her belly. She pulled him towards her and Valston collapsed on top of her, his cock shriveling up and his come starting to leak out of her worn cunt. They both rose out of the bathtub and surveyed the bathroom. It was worse now, with even more water splashed all over the place. Valston extended his hand to Karen and helped her out of the tub.

"Massage satisfactory?" he asked as they walked into the bedroom.

"Massage satisfactory," Karen grinned, patting his well-muscled young backside.

"I'm going to go an' get a mop, clean up the bathroom," Valston said, as he scooped up his shorts and wiggled back into them and trotted from the bedroom.

The blush which had spread throughout Karen's body was beginning to subside and now she went prowling through the house. As good as young Valston had been in the saddle, Karen felt that his banging had only been a preliminary fuck. Her body had been tuned to a fine point and now Karen was ready for a really heavy evening.

She headed for Meredith's room and seeing that the door was open she poked her head into it and was surprised by what she saw. She'd caught Meredith with Thelma, and as she watched from behind the doorpost, she became increasingly fascinated. Thelma had stripped off her frock and now lay back on the bed. Although she was tall and her body stout, she moved with grace and sensuality. She lay back and propped a pillow under her hips raising them and then lifted her head. From behind the door Karen couldn't see Meredith but she had an incredible view of Thelma's body. Thelma had large thick legs that were firm as rocks. They were almost straight up in the air and spread wide apart, exposing her little ebony asshole and the thick patch of tight curls that were even darker than her skin. The dense thatch had a part in it and through the part Karen could see the thick pink lips, almost as thick as the lips of Thelma's mouth, poking through the black forest of her crotch.

Karen could see the little droplets of juice clinging to the luscious lips. There was a big grin on her face as she lay there waggling her legs silently, digging her ass into the pillow.

Karen admired the two large buttocks on which Thelma balanced herself as she squirmed. They were large and fleshy, yet somehow very sexy. Karen looked up beyond the buttocks, over the big hairy gash upon her attention had been riveted, and looked at the big round belly. Yes, it was fat, but somehow it was also magnificent and firm and Karen felt an unexpected twinge of lust. She wanted that large, fat woman, wanted to bury her head in the folds of fat that seemed to have remained firm, wanted to stick her head through the hair bush and into the wet, pink crevice. She wanted to throw herself on that big fleshy, beckoning body. Karen looked at the large tits that had earlier been straining against the frock that now lay on the floor. The tits were also superbly fleshy and rolled back and forth from side to side and from front to back, with the big black areolas and nipples at their centres.

"Hey, Massa Meredith, you come hump me now?" Thelma called out.

Without a word, Meredith appeared in Karen's field of vision, walking from a corner of the bedroom to where his housekeeper lay with her legs waving in the air. Meredith was nude and jiggled slightly as he walked, but one thing was very clear. His big cock was already erect and it preceded him as he approached his big black partner.

"Open wide, Thelma, my love," he whispered, "because here I come."

Karen fingered her crevice, toying with the hair at the entrance. She wanted Meredith. She wanted that big stiff cock inside of her, plunging in and driving her insane. She needed it. She wanted the big black woman lying on the bed awaiting the man she served. She wanted to roll over that big, fleshy black body, smooth and silky, but soft and welcoming.

Karen buried her fingers deeper into her cave and wiggled them back and forth as she watched Meredith kneel on the edge of the bed and Thelma spreading her legs even wider as Meredith leaned against the V of her legs and steadied himself as he maneuvered his cock right on target through the pink portals and into the palace of flesh.

"*Ahhhhhh!*" Thelma moaned long and low. It was a combination sigh and gurgle as Meredith's rod slid home deep into the hot furnace of her waiting cunt. Thelma tossed her hips up, bouncing Meredith into the air so that his cock would come down again and hammer into her hole. Meredith pulled back and then slammed forward. Their bodies made a slap-slap sound as Meredith slammed down and Thelma heaved up, working in unison together toward orgasm.

Karen turned for a moment and saw Valston heading for her room with a mop and bucket to clean up the leftovers of their little humping session in the bathtub. In the background she continued to hear the slap-slap of the two bodies meeting in love.

Karen turned back to the duo in the master bedroom and she could see that they were both climaxing, wordlessly quivering and shooting their loads as their bodies strained against each other in that cosmic moment of utter bliss.

"Well, Karen, are you coming in or are you just going to stand there or are you going to join us?" Meredith called out as he rolled off Thelma, exposing once again her juicy body.

"Huh?"

"We've both been watching you for a long time," Meredith laughed. "Come on and join us." He patted the mattress on the other side of his fat black lover.

Karen smiled. Lucky Meredith has a sense of humour, she thought, as she walked into the room and plunked down beside Thelma.

"Miss Karen, darlin', would you like to suck my boobie?" Thelma asked magnanimously.

"How did you know?" Karen responded. "Your eyes are open as big as my boobies, that be why, child, go ahead suck, Mama Thelma now," she replied.

Karen bent over and took a large mouthful of Thelma's ample tit. It tasted sweet-sour from the sweat of humping, but it was big and soft and Karen loved it.

"Now don't get too excited, Karen," Meredith cut in. "There are some people coming over for a little party later, and I've got one friend picked out just for you."

"Why, thank you," Karen responded. "I'm looking forward to it."

"Thelma, go get her the special salve,"

Meredith commanded.

Thelma was enjoying Karen's little sucking session as much as Karen was, but she reluctantly got up. She pulled her skimpy frock onto her body and left the room.

Meredith reached over and fondled Karen's tits.

"The locals have an amazing collections of potions," he said, pushing her boobs together so he nipples touched and grew erect under the pressure. "Anyway, the one I sent Thelma for is guaranteed to net you any man you want and if you'll take my advice, set your aim at Larry, huh?"

"For at least one night," Karen laughed, pressing up against Meredith's hands as he applied a little pressure to her tender boobs.

"Enjoying yourself so far?" Meredith asked.

"Yes, especially that little houseboy of yours," she said, rolling over on top of Meredith and straddling his body.

Meredith looked up as Karen balanced herself across his stomach and moving back so that her ass slithered over his stomach. His cock grew erect and her ass slithered over it, too, and she spread her legs so that it could slide into her waiting crevice, which was sopping wet with anticipation. Karen groaned in ecstasy as Meredith's powerful cock went home, and she rode up and down, up and down hard on the granite-hard prick that was poking deep into her.

Meredith lay back and laughed as Karen rode and rode and rode until she keeled over into a sort of orgasmic paralysis, her body shaking and quivering as Meredith's tool shot his load deep into her.

Chapter 8

Karen awoke with a start, feeling a pair of strong large hands lifting her buttocks. She was lying on her belly and the hands turned her on her back. Karen blinked her eyes open and looked up to see Thelma leaning over, her tits straining against her flimsy frock.

"Wake up, Miss Karen," she cooed. "Guests be arrivin' and we must be puttin' dat potion on."

Karen rolled over and surrendered to the strong hands of Thelma. She would rather have taken Thelma off to her own room and spent a couple of hours exploring her big, black body with its many contrasts, large, but delicate, fleshy, yet firm and oh, so, so sexy.

Karen propped herself up on one arm and watched as Thelma kneeled at the foot of the bed and whispered what seemed to be a prayer. Thelma swiftly arose and took a small vial from her pocket and poured a bit of the creamy liquid into the palm of her hand and slapped it over Karen's left tit. Karen winced under the sudden impact, but the liquid seemed to be warm and soothing and besides, Thelma's hand was so comforting. Thelma repeated the procedure with Karen's other tit and again Karen felt heat spreading through her body, just like the gradual budding of a really great orgasm.

Thelma was really enjoying her work and the smile on her face showed it. She spilled the remainder of the vial on Karen's belly and massaged it thoroughly in, from the bottom of her tits into the dense bush between her legs.

"Bring good luck to your pretty body, child," Thelma grinned at Karen, her strong white teeth literally lighting up her face.

Karen smiled back and spread her legs, inviting Thelma, but Thelma frowned.

"Sorry darlin', not when guests are here," she said suddenly, giving her a final pat, then turning and leaving the room.

Karen surveyed her body. The white cream had disappeared into her skin and she ran her hands over her tits and belly feeling the unusual silky feeling that her skin had gained from the cream.

"You must be Karen," a voice from beyond the door called out. Karen wasn't really startled. She somehow expected someone to walk through the door, and now he did.

Tall and blond with a well-toned torso and Karen could see almost every one of the bulging muscles. He was clad only in a pair of flowered beach shorts and obviously loved showing off his perfect body.

"I'm Larry."

"They told me a lot about you," Karen replied.

"What did they say?" he shot back looking over Karen who made no effort to rise or hide any part of her body that lay sprawled on the bed before him like a delicious platter of goodies.

"Just that I had to meet you, though they didn't say why," Karen answered, rearranging herself slightly so he could have a better view of her pussy.

"They told me quite a bit about you, too."

"What?"

"Ah, now *that* would be telling," he grinned, approaching the bed.

"Well, why don't you check it out for yourself?"

Larry said nothing, just stood there, fiddling with the stretch band on his shorts and watching as Karen rolled over and tossed her hair back and forth making a long, whipping motion with it. Karen knew that cream or no cream, magic or no magic, she had Larry in the palm of her hand and she was enjoying the sensation. She kneeled on the bed, drawing herself up and then fell back into a complete split, her cunt opening wide as the muscles stretched her lips open. Grasping her ankles, Karen held her legs wide apart, so Larry could get a solid view of her sexy, yawning crevice.

"Everything they said about you was true," he laughed out loud.

"Everything they said and more," Karen grinned back. "Watch this."

Karen pulled herself back to a standing position and then leaped off the bed, landing on her hands and going into a full cartwheel.

"And this," she continued.

Now she arched her back, her legs spread wide. She fell back, bending in half backwards. This incredible trick stunned even Larry. He stared motionless at Karen who jiggled her tits which hung back down towards her shoulders now. He also stared at Karen's bush, which was stretched tight by this latest contortion. Her cunt lips poked through the thick black hair and at the top of her cunt, the pink knob of her clit pushed through like a miniature prick. Larry's mouth watered as he surveyed the display of luscious female genitalia before him, and slipped his shorts over his stiff rod and down his legs.

"Don't just stand there, lover boy," Karen

laughed, jiggling her tits again. "Come hump me."

Larry knew an invitation when he received one and took two steps toward Karen. He fingered her patch and ran his fingers up and down the ridge of her cunt lips, feeling the heat and the thick, crystal-clear cunt-juice that oozed out between them.

"Do it now, you bastard," Karen hissed.

Holding his cock and sliding it toward the centre of the soft, gooey slit, Larry stepped forward and pushed hard. He didn't expect his cock to slide home so easily, but the magic cream must have been doing its thing because Karen's cunt reacted like a vacuum cleaner, sucking it right in and gripping it hard.

Larry reached down to Karen's shoulders and brought her up to a standing position.

"Thanks," she breathed. "My back was beginning to feel it."

Larry made no response. His cock was still in her and now he pressed his lips against hers and pried her mouth open with his tongue and plunged it deep into her throat. Karen responded by sucking his tongue into her and chewing on it. She wrapped her arms around him and hoisted herself onto his body, wrapping her legs around his torso. His pole felt good inside her and she wiggled up and down as shivers of pleasure raced through her body.

Karen's weight caused Larry to stumble and waver, but he tensed his muscles and staggered to the bed where he fell down on top of her, plunging his pole even deeper into her. Karen let out a sharp gasp as she felt his cock drill deep into her. It was more than she had bargained for, but she liked the sensation of such deep and total penetration.

The two rolled back and forth on the bed, over and around, play-wrestling. Karen struggled atop Larry and tried to pin him. Larry allowed himself to be pinned only because he liked to have a bitch like Karen riding him, slamming her body against his, her tits bouncing madly against his chest and her cunt clutching at his long, erect cock.

When Larry tired of this, he rolled over on top of Karen and started giving her the riding of her life up and down, up and down, slapping his chest against hers as hard as he could, knocking the wind from her lungs.

"Come on, baby, come on," Larry cried as he felt his cock begin to pulsate in her tight cunt.

Karen let her body swing free, her sex in tune with his cock, her pussy juice sloshing around inside the passionate vessel of her cunt. At last she let loose and allowed herself to come, shutting her eyes so tight that she could see stars as she felt the shock waves course through her body. Larry laughed as he felt her body go stiff and then launched his own wad deep into her. This set Karen off again and even Larry's body pinning Karen's to the bed failed to hold her down, as she bucked and twisted, tossing him off her and onto the bed next to her.

"They didn't tell me the good bits about you, Larry said, grinning at Karen and fondling her tits as she came down off her high.

"You better believe it," she said, bounding up and taking his hand and dragging him toward the hallway.

"Let's get into a scene with someone else," Karen said. "I gotta have more."

"If the little lady wants more, she's gonna get more," Larry said, laughing and following Karen. He was thoroughly satisfied by this superwoman, but if she wanted more, he was going to join her.

Karen didn't know how Larry would react to her little scheme, but she dragged him along anyway.

Fuck it! Karen thought, I just gotta have Thelma and if he doesn't like it, he can fuck himself. Karen had been aching for Thelma all afternoon but events had conspired to keep them apart. Larry and Karen wandered down the hall. They caught a glimpse of Meredith slipping it to Liz, whose body was painted with bright orange and purple paints. Crazy girl! thought Karen. The two were so involved with each other that they didn't even notice Karen and Larry heading down the hallway.

Karen led Larry to the kitchen where Thelma was bent over her work. Karen left Larry at the door and tiptoed into the kitchen. She gently approached Thelma from the rear and carefully placed her hands on Thelma's hips and squeezed gently.

Thelma turned around with a start.

"Oh, it's you!" shrieked the cheerful black woman. "Hello, Miss Karen."

"Come join us on the beach."

"Oh, no, Miss Karen. Master M needs me here."

"I need you on the beach," Karen said, lifting Thelma's frock and massaging the valley between her immense buttocks. "Come with us."

"Oh, no, Miss Karen, oh, no," Thelma repeated, but this time less certainly as she started to feel the effects of Karen's hands kneading the flesh behind her twat.

Larry watched from the doorway and he, too, grew fascinated by the lovely contrast between Karen and the black woman to whom she was ministering. Thelma was glorious. She seemed to be all things, fat and solid, yet strangely sexy and alluring all at the same time. From behind, Larry could see the edges of her tits quiver as Karen pressed her body against the big woman's back all the time continuing her massage and still whispering in her ear.

"Come on, Thelma, come on, let's go."

"No, I mustn't."

"Yes, damnit, Thelma, yes."

"No, please, no."

"Yes, Thelma, yes."

Karen's voice grew more and more insistent and her hand motions stronger and faster. Thelma's voice grew weaker and weaker as she leaned against Karen and fell under the spell of her massage.

Suddenly, Thelma's body shook violently, almost pushing Karen's body away. Thelma gripped the edge of the table and held tight as she came shuddering and twitching. She turned around showing her front. There was a big round wet spot at her crotch from the pussy juice that poured out of her hole. The wet spot on the dress clung against her twat highlighting her kinky cunt hair that pressed out through the flimsy cotton.

"Oh, now heavens child, look what you did to my dress," she complained smiling. "I must go change now so Master Meredith won't see me like this."

"I'll buy you a dozen like them," Larry said, stepping out from the doorway and smiling at the big woman, "if you'll join us on the beach."

Thelma stared at him, tall and white,

Orgy Girl ★ 171

standing before her with his full erection. She looked at Karen who smiled and nodded. Now Karen knew that she had indeed met Mr. Right – that she and Larry would be happy together for a long time.

"Okay," Thelma said meekly, breaking into a huge grin.

Karen took her by one hand and Larry by the other and they led her out the kitchen door and down to the beach behind one of the many dunes that dotted it. Karen stopped Thelma and stepped in front of her and sank to her knees. Thelma knew what was expected of her, and was even looking forward to it. She spread her legs, causing her frock to rise up her hips. Karen pushed her head under the frock and started licking Thelma's patch clean. There were little droplets of come speckled through her hair and Karen was rubbing her chin and running her tongue through the black forest.

Larry unbuttoned Thelma's frock and pulled it over her head setting her tits free. The sight of those tits jiggling so sensuously drove Larry wild. He stepped behind the big black woman and anchored himself to those tits with his hands, pushing them from side to side and puffing them every which way. They were like firm jelly in his hands and the sensation drove him wild. His cock was aching and now he pressed it against her ass, feeling the knot of muscles pressing back against his glans relax and contract in mute invitation. He leaned harder as he felt Thelma pressing back against him. She wanted his cock up her ass and he was going to shove it in. Karen was slurping and gobbling and Thelma started to pant under her assault.

"Push, Mr. Larry, push," Thelma instructed him urgently.

Larry applied himself once more, gripping her tits and sharply bringing his hips forward, hammering his prick into her. Thelma let out a long, low moan as she felt the buggering cock slide into her. She wasn't sure whether she was moaning because of Karen's attack or Larry's cock. Karen let up for a moment and Thelma started falling forward on all fours, landing on her hands and knees. Karen squirmed under her, and Larry continued his assault, slapping his hips against the ample, well-padded buttocks.

Thelma lay down atop Karen as Larry continued cornholing the big black woman. Karen felt almost squashed under the two bodies but Thelma's body was so warm and all-encompassing that she hardly minded the weight.

Larry started to feel himself come and Thelma knew that any moment now her ass would be filled with his reservoir of come. She straightened up knocking Larry flat on his back. His cock waved wildly in the air back and forth, but Thelma squirmed around, forgetting Karen, and grabbed it in her fist and started bringing him off.

He squirted his come onto his own belly and was immediately attacked by both women who started licking through the blond hair on his stomach and chest, licking up his sweet, juicy come.

Thelma tongued his entire body, while Karen sucked his cock in her mouth, up and down the now-limp member which eventually grew stiff again.

"Ride me, ride me," Larry gasped.

Thelma continued to lick but Karen quickly mounted Larry and rode him like she never rode before, up and down his pole, though this time neither of them came.

* * *

They had returned to the house with Thelma, and since the others had gone island hopping in Meredith's big boat, they had enjoyed a leisurely lunch served by Valston and cooked by his mother. It was delicious – but then Karen had expected that Thelma would be a natural cook from the sensual ways of the big woman. They had returned to the beach and now the two lovers lay naked, arm in arm while the sun sank lower and lower in the sky.

"Come with me Karen," Larry began as he fondled her luscious tits.

"Maybe. Where to?"

"Paris. You'll be the toast of the town. I've a nice apartment and – oh – plenty of friends who'd love to hump you. I'll pay for everything – we'll go by boat and screw all the way there."

"Sounds pretty good, lover."

Larry rolled over onto Karen. His cock was stiff again and he was aching to give this beautiful girl a proper pronging.

Karen brought her knees up and spread her thighs and was rewarded by the feel of his cock sliding along the soft flesh of her inner thigh. She felt the hot head of it slide higher and higher and she felt the tremors of passion and lust increase within her as the cock made its way to her cunt. Her pussy was wet and becoming wetter and wetter with the flow of twat-juice that was gushing out of her and making her slick and ready for fucking. The pleasure she felt at the touch of Larry's cock was something wonderful and she knew that she could be very happy with him.

"Fuck me, Larry. Fuck me hard, please – do it – really stick your cock up my cunt," she gasped as he thrust harder and higher into her tight young pussy.

The luscious and delicious feelings she felt

were something that she could not get enough of and she knew that when they got to Paris this would continue for as long as they were both willing. She felt this and she wanted to continue to fuck him for the rest of her life.

Her thighs were spread as far as they would go and she bucked her hips up to get more and more of his cock into her cunt. It was thick and solid and completely filled up her hole. She raked and scraped his tool across her clit and vibrated with the intensity of the emotions she felt. Her cunt oozed and spewed forth come and juices and she gave him all the cunt and the pleasure that he wanted and more. Larry plunged and shoved his cock as far as it would go and she clenched the muscles of her cunt to envelope the shaft in tight, sweet meat.

"Do it slow," she gasped as he stroked up and down above her.

Then she shifted her weight. She turned him quickly around and got on top of him. She was now sitting on his pole and rising up and down on it with all the force and the pressure she could.

It was sheer heaven to her and she loved every inch and every stroke of his cock in and out of her. Her mouth was hanging half open and she bounced harder on his cock and controlled the delicious sensations that she felt. Her tits jiggled up and down with the force of her fucking and she leant back and raked her fingernails across his balls. He moaned and groaned beneath her as Karen found the crack of his ass with her fingers and plunged deeper in there.

She felt the tight hot feeling of his asshole and she intuitively knew that he loved this. Karen knew that this was driving him out of his mind and making him tremble and twitch with the pleasure and the pain of their fucking and plunging. As his cock rammed in and out of her, she raked her own fingers over her engorged clit and stimulated herself at the same time.

Her clit was hard and erect and she felt the little nubbin of her pleasure come to flaming life beneath the loving affections of her fingers. There was nothing left to do now but to come. She felt the waves of pleasure about to break over her and make her shoot the cream that was within her. Her cunt throbbed and pulsated and her head span with the pleasure she felt. The intense enjoyment of her orgasm made Karen gasp. She felt her cunt tighten up and then flood around the shaft of his manhood, soaking his tightened scrotal sac.

Larry was about to come as well. He raked his cock in and out of her and then, geyser-like, shot an incredible amount of come deep into her very womb. She could not believe the amount of goo that he shot into her: it came dribbling out of her hole and coursed down her thighs. She drenched his entire pubic area until both their bushes were matted with gooey white cum. They were happy and exhausted and she collapsed on top of him laughing...

"That was the best ever..."

"Funny, I was about to say the same."

They both knew that they had been hornier than they had ever been with anyone else and the novelty and the thrill of this discovery simply made them want each other even more. They had fucked on the beach like a couple of romantic maniacs who just could not get enough of the wonderful pleasures they were able to give one another. A tropical storm was gathering with dark, rolling thunderclouds, and huge warm raindrops fell heavily on their tired bodies but they didn't care. They had their own hurricane of lust to occupy them. So they just lay on the beach and let the gentle waves wash over them as they stroked and kissed like old lovers.

Chapter 9

A few days later both Larry and Karen were ready to leave. They said goodbye to everybody and a couple of days later they were on the boat to France. It was the first time that Karen had been to Europe and the idea of this trip was utterly thrilling to her. She was wildly excited. Larry and she fucked every way possible in their comfortable stateroom. The weather wasn't particularly good, so they would often order their meals by room service to have in their cabin, enjoying the food half naked, playing and eating at the same time.

For Karen it was the start of a great adventure. She wanted to be a Bohemian in the worst way possible. From what she'd read it seemed to her that any other place was just a pale imitation of that kind of life. Paris was the only place to do it– Paris was the real thing.

All of the hip and the freaky people that she had met in New York came from there and she knew that she would fit right in with the sort of life style they led.

Her cunt couldn't wait either.

It was Larry's fault, really. He had told her

so much about Paris that she had already been there in her mind. The bars, the restaurants, the crowded Metro, the art galleries and the hip art movements that seemed to spring up at the drop of a hat. Artists, writers, musicians – creative people, Larry had said, you know the types.

Yes, Karen thought, she knew those types all right, and she knew that this would suit her just fine, because where there were those sort of people, there would also be a lot of fucking.

She knew that her orgiastic existence wouldn't cease when they got there and that Larry wouldn't mind if she went off and fucked anybody she wanted. In fact no one would be there to stop her from having the kind of hedonistic fun that she had always craved and somehow – at this stage of her life – needed more than anything else in the world.

She was glad that Larry was like that and relieved that the arrangement was perfectly reciprocal – if Larry wanted to go out and screw some girl without asking her first – well, fine! If this goose was getting her sauce, it seemed only fair that the gander should get his…

Despite their cabin fun, it seemed to her that the boat took forever to get to its destination. It seemed to them both like they'd been sailing for weeks when finally the coast of France was there. Neither of them could wait to get off the boat and start their adventure together.

They boarded the train to Paris and Karen spent most of her time gazing out the window at the strange new landscape that greeted her. Larry slept for most of the ride and Karen found herself becoming bored and restless. There was something brewing within her and at first she did not know what it was.

She was beginning to feel really horny. Karen knew the symptoms, just as she knew that there was only one real cure for this state of mind. She had to get laid and she had to do it right away.

She looked around her to see if there might be any likely looking males with whom she could fuck. She was incredibly curious about all the stories she had heard about Frenchmen being such great lovers, and she knew that there was only one way to find out – find one to fuck.

The idea of finding some guy – any guy who was OK-looking and French – and having him fuck her just like that flared brightly in her imagination and soon the temptation became an obsessive imperative that she could no longer resist. She smiled to herself and shifted her thighs; this small body movement made her realise that her pussy was growing extremely wet and she crossed her thighs in such a way that her labia and clitoris, now slick with oozing juices, were delightfully stimulated.

Karen was hot.

But the only person she saw that might fit her needs was the young conductor who came around and checked tickets and announced destinations. He reminded her a little of Errol Flynn in those old black and white movies, with his cheeky smile and cute little moustache. She already knew that he was likely to have a thick cock from the impressive bulge she saw in his tight pants. She was willing and hungry and more than prepared to try anything that he might want to do. So the next time he came around she gave him a big smile and asked him something in the little French she knew.

He smiled at her and replied in English.

"I understand English, young lady," he said to her.

"I'm so glad. I wanted to know where the bathroom is."

"Come with me. I will show you a bathroom that is proper – I mean, clean. The public ones are not fit for pigs. I will let you use the private one we have for special passengers and for the staff."

Karen hoped that she would have the chance to fuck him and she also hoped that she would be able to communicate to him the need she had for his cock. He led the way through the cars and then finally stopped before a wood panelled door. He opened it and stepped inside. He began showing her where the things were and was about to leave when she lifted her skirt and pulled down her panties. The door was still closed and the knob was still in his hand when he whirled around to catch sight of her doing that.

"You are very... how do you say... brave." he said casually.

"What do you mean?" Karen replied in as insouciant a tone as she could.

"When a woman does certain things, acts in a certain way, then a man may perhaps receive the wrong idea as to her intentions."

"Any intentions you have are fine with me, honey," she smiled at him as her hands slowly picked up her skirt and her fingers tangled themselves in the fine down of her crotch. Her middle finger gently caressed her clit and a shudder of pleasure shot through her, and she let out a shaky little sigh.

She closed her eyes and bit her lower lip in delicious pleasure as the conductor looked on.

"No. I apologize. I am being foolish. A man could only get one impression from what you are doing, Mam'selle."

He approached her after locking the door behind him. She heard the click and, with a sudden thrill, she knew that they would definitely fuck now. His hands reached out and joined hers as she stroked and fingered her cunt. She felt the dry warmth of his hands on hers and pushed deeper into her cunt.

He pulled her hands away and then he continued stroking at her clit and her cunt lips. Karen could not believe the incredible passion she suddenly felt as his hands found the lips and spread them slowly apart. She moaned low in her throat and smiled while her eyes closed.

"Nice. Oh yes, that's right, do it slowly. Nice and slow."

Karen could tell that his hands were experienced and that he knew just what to do to get her hot and excited. She spread her legs a little farther apart and let his fingers explore every part of her thighs and her cunt. She leaned closer to him because she could hardly stand any more. Her legs were weak and rubbery and she gasped as his middle finger found her cunt hole and dived into the moistening and thickening tissues.

He prodded harder and then she had to sit. She could no longer stand. She leaned towards him and he picked her up and sat her bare ass on the cool porcelain of the wash basin.

She felt the contrast of his hot fingers and her hot cunt with the coldness of the sink and a shudder of pleasure shot through her and made her pant and gasp in delicious abandon.

Her cunt was hot and flaming and the cream oozed out of her and dripped to the sink below her. Her cunt could not get enough of his meaty fingers inside her and Karen knew that her cunt needed his cock.

"You lovely beast. Do it slow and easy. Nice and slow," she moaned as her chin lifted and her mouth hung open a little more now. Her eyes were closed, and she revelled in the sublime feelings his hand and his fingers were giving her.

He had two fingers inside her and stroked slowly but forcefully and raked his knuckles across her clit. The sensations she was having were driving her mad and Karen now wanted his cock. She could feel the meaty tool beneath the fabric of his pants and she stroked it with her hand.

"I want this," she gasped.

"*Mais, oui, Ma'mselle. Avec plaisir!,*" he answered grinning. Such a gent, she thought. Why, he's even helping me improve my French!

He quickly undid the zipper and the buckle of the pants and his cock sprang suddenly to life. It bobbed up and down before her and she grasped the head of it with her little fist. The man groaned as he felt the cool fingers surround the head of his cock and shoved it a little in and out of her palm.

They were both hotter than hell and they

struggled against each other to battle for the best position.

"Fuck me now," she moaned urgently as her hands pulled his cock to her.

She felt the tool approach her cunt and she spread her cunt lips with her hands to get the shaft in there. She craved him more than anything now and she knew that this would be one fuck that she would not forget. She wrapped her legs around his waist and pulled him closer and closer to her until she could feel the head of his cock pressed against her cunt lips. The steady rocking motion of the train made it even more delightful. He knew what he was doing. His technique was making her squirm and tremble with delight.

He rubbed the head of his thick cock against her cunt lips and she experienced a rush of pleasure that made her scream a little.

"You like, no?" he asked.

"I like, yes. Very much," Karen gasped as she felt the head of his cock now enter her cunt and slide into the already wet and slick cunt hole.

She felt the shaft of it penetrate all the way to the depths of her and knew that he was one hell of a fucker. She knew that he was good at what he did and she bucked her hips to him to get more and more of his cock into her. The white porcelain was now wet with the juices of their love as she rocked her cunt back and forth on his cock. She felt the tool pulsate and throb inside her and she knew that she was going to come soon.

The train passed over some points and the jolting added extra spice to his thrusts and plunges while Karen clawed his stomach and his ass lightly with her nails.

She drummed her feet on the back of his thighs and squeezed his rock-hard asscheeks, urging him to fuck harder and faster.

"Come on and do it fast now. *Plus vite!* Ohhh, yes, now that's so gooooood!"

He plunged and shoved his shaft in and out between her cunt lips and drove the head of it as far as it would go into her cunt. She was in ecstasy now – Karen was panting heavily and he could see little beads of sweat breaking out on her forehead.

Now she raked her fingernails along the bottom of his balls. They were panting and gasping; she could tell that they were climbing towards the inevitable conclusion of their wild, uninhibited fuck as she felt the first tremors of her orgasm. Now they both fucked like a couple of rutting animals.

Her bare ass on that porcelain sink was becoming wet and slick and she was having a hard time staying on there. With a hand on each buttock, he picked her up and lifted her into the air. Karen was now completely impaled on his cock and she rode it like she would a horse. Her cunt was now streaming with come. It was oozing with the wonderful female juices of her pussy and she drenched his cock and his balls with it. Irrationally, she thought about the mess it would make of his impeccably smart uniform.

Karen knew that she was now ready to come. She felt the pressure increase and grow in her and about to burst forth with all the restrained craziness that was in her. She wanted them to come together. But it was not to be, and Karen could not wait.

"I'm coming, I'm coming," she gasped. "Now... now!" She realised that she did not even know this man's name. "That was brilliant, Monsieur, but what about you? You haven't come!"

She disentangled herself from him and she went about the tiny cubicle picking up odd bits of clothing.

"What about you?" she repeated as he stood in front of her holding his cock and jerking it slowly... he looked almost in pain.

She slipped into her panties and smiled at him. Then she ducked down and took the tight, quivering head of his cock into her soft, wet, warm mouth. She reached under it and squeezed his tight balls. That's all it took. The man came like a fire hydrant... she counted the spurts – there were eight in all.

Her mouth was full of his gluey sperm. She swallowed and licked her lips.

"Wow! That was sensational! Maybe I'll see you in Paris."

"Perhaps, Mam'selle. I certainly hope so. It would be *mon plaisir.*"

"Mine too, hon!"

He approached her and kissed her hand. She had not expected anything so charming as that and somehow it ended the whole thing on a light and delightful note. She knew hat she had pleased him but he could have easily just turned off the charm as soon as he had shot his load, she thought. Instead he had acted like some gallant officer in the Foreign Legion and she half-expected him to click his heels before they cautiously emerged from the little cubicle.

Karen returned to Larry and snuggled close beside him on the seat. He was still asleep and had not missed her absence. Even if he had been awake she was sure that she would have done the same thing. She would even have told him about it.

She rode in silence all the way to Paris and Larry slept soundly. Karen awoke him just as the train pulled into the terminal and began to gather their things. They took a cab to a small pension. Larry said it would be just for a few days as his apartment was being redecorated. They began to unpack

Orgy Girl ★ 189

and go through the motions of getting their life started in this foreign city.

Larry seemed to know all the places and she let him make all the decisions for the first few days. But for some reason the polish and the novelty of Larry began to wear thin. She could no longer be as excited and thrilled at his touch as she had been back at Meredith's place. At one point he admitted to her that the apartment was not really his and that its lender had come back at an inopportune moment.

There was something stirring in her that she knew he could not satisfy and Karen wanted to shake free of Larry. She needed space. She wanted time on her own.

In the days that followed she met all of Larry's friends and felt the same things about them. They were mostly all Americans who had notions of being artists and bohemians. They considered themselves the new wave of expatriates, following in the footsteps of Hemingway and Toklas, Stein and Fitzgerald. But she could see them for what they really were, spoiled middle class children that had never fully grown up, and with money to burn, mostly their parents' money. They were largely untalented poseurs, she thought.

All but one of them gave her that impression. She seemed to sense an authenticity and a genuine soul searching quality in a painter called David. He seemed different from the rest. He didn't go and party at the drop of a hat like the rest of them. He seemed harder working, more remote and reflective. Not a party person really – more a 'penseur' than a poseur. She preferred that.

Her social life with Larry was now almost exclusively spent with this circle of friends. And she used every opportunity to see David whenever they went out.

In the evenings they would gather at a cafe and while away the hours drinking wine and Pernod. In these conversations David would usually remain silent. Karen could see the slight contempt he had for most of them. She could see the way he looked almost embarrassed at some of their immature statements and ridiculous theorizing.

She knew him for what he was: a real person.

All the others now seemed pale imitations of real and genuinely interesting people. They were posturing fools that wanted people to judge them on what they appeared to be rather than what they genuinely were.

One night as they sat at the cafe Larry drank so much that he got completely shit-faced.

He could hardly walk and Karen was left with the chore of taking him home. She knew that she could not manage alone and she was immediately offered help by all of his friends. David offered too but not as forcefully as the others. She wanted to be taken home by David. She knew that the other men only wanted to get into her pants and fuck. That was all right with her but she didn't want to fuck with any of them. They would bore her to tears with idle chatter and ridiculous attempts at getting her to bed.

They rode in the cab with Larry by the window and the two of them pressed together.

She could feel a crackle of electricity in the air between them. Karen knew what it was and it utterly thrilled her. She felt the same things he did at that moment and suddenly she just knew that he had wanted her all this time as much as she had wanted him. She felt her cunt come alive, starting to juice. She clamped her legs together in case it started to give out an odour that would betray her, but this action only made things worse. She was sure that he could smell her delicious cuntal emanations.

"How long have you been in Paris?" Karen asked, trying to make innocuous conversation.

"Three years."

"That's a long time. Do you miss America?"

"Not a bit. I hate that place."

"Why?"

"It's too boring. I have my reasons."

"I'd like to hear them."

"Are you sure?"

"Yes. I think you're far more interesting than all the other people back there."

"Thanks. I think you're pretty interesting too."

"You didn't have to say that just because I said it, I wasn't fishing for compliments, David."

He smiled.

"I know. I still think you're interesting."

"When can I hear your reasons?" she said after a while.

"Anytime Larry says it's alright."

"He doesn't own me you know. I can make up my own mind."

"That's not the way it looks to me. I think he sort of dominates you a little."

Her voice rose indignantly.

"That's not so. Not at all. I do what I want"

"Ah... the lady doth protest too much! Perhaps there's some truth in what I just said."

Karen blushed. She knew she could hide nothing from him. He was far too wise and worldly not to know when things were right and when they were not.

She could feel the power and the assertion in him when he said that.

"I'll be going away in a few days. I guess we'll see each other when I come back."

"When are you coming back?"

"In a week. I must see a friend."

A woman, Karen thought. She thought he must have dozens of women stashed around all over France. He seemed the quiet type that would have a stable of women to keep him happy.

"He's a guitar maker. At least eighty years old and still making guitars as if he were twenty."

She breathed a sigh of relief not even knowing why she was happy that he did not have another woman.

"He sounds interesting."

"To say the least. He cuts his own trees and saws his own wood for the guitars."

"Where are you going?"

"To Spain. Just across the border actually."

"I wish I could go. I mean I wish I could get away from Paris for a while and see the rest of Europe as long as I'm here."

"Would you like to go with me?"

She was taken aback by this. She had thought that David, despite his interest, had been taking things slowly. She wanted to go more than anything but she was sure that Larry would not let her go. He would make a fuss about it and refuse to let her go.

They arrived at the pension where Larry and Karen stayed and David helped her take the limp and drunken body of Larry up the stairs and into bed.

"Well, thanks a lot, David," Karen said as she shook his hand at the door.

"Anytime. If you need me for anything just call. Here's my number at home and at work."

"Alright. I'll do that."

That night Karen could hardly sleep. She felt something stirring and moving within her. She felt the presence of David all around her as if he were a spectre. It was as if his ethereal spirit had somehow penetrated her and discovered the deepest secrets of her soul.

She knew it was odd for her to feel this way and she knew she was treading on dangerous ground with this man. Yet she could not help feeling the way she did.

The next day Larry could hardly get out of bed. He was sick and weak and could hardly move.

"Man. Have I got a hangover."

"You shouldn't drink so much. You know you can't hold it."

"I can too. It was just that lousy cheese I ate. It must have been spoiled."

"Everybody else ate it. Nobody got sick."

"They're used to it, Karen. They've been in Paris longer and they can take it. Bacteria and all that."

"Yeah. I guess you're right."

She knew that it was not the cheese or anything else. It was the fact that Larry had been digging a grave for himself and he had taken to drinking to blot out the mess he was in.

"Listen, Larry. I want to tell you something. I want to go away with David. He's going to Spain for a week and I want to go with him." The shock registered slowly on his face. She could see that he was hurt but she had to fight for her own salvation. She couldn't stand around and be sucked into the same private hell that Larry was going through.

"So go," he said angrily. "It doesn't matter to me what the hell you do and I don't give a shit who you fuck."

"Don't be like that, Larry. Please don't make a scene. Can't you just once accept life for what it is and stop crying like a baby every time something happens that you don't like? Face it Larry. You're a child."

Larry limply lay back on the bed and closed his eyes.

"Sure. Whatever. So go! Just when I needed you the most."

He couldn't resist getting in that blackmailing little dig at her.

"You don't need me Larry. You need a mother."

She whirled on her heels and went into

the other room to begin packing her things.

As she packed she made a phone call to David.

"Hello, David. This is Karen. Is that invitation still open to go to Spain?"

"Yes it is. How did Larry take it?"

"Badly."

"I knew he would."

"He'll learn I suppose. One of these days he'll learn."

"Shall I come by and pick you up?"

"No. I want to take a cab. I want to do this my way."

"Alright. Ring for me when you get here and I'll come down and meet you. We'll have lunch at the station and then well take the afternoon train."

"Yes. That's fine."

"I'll see you later."

She hung up and continued to pack. Larry stumbled into the room. His dressing gown flopped about him limply.

"When did this all happen?" he asked.

"Last night. When he helped me take you home."

"When the cat's away huh?"

"No. Not when the cat's away, Larry. When the cat is there, and all but insensible with drink. And stop trying to make me sound like a slut or a whore."

"Well, isn't that just what you are?"

"No, Honey. Really, it's you who are the whore. You sell your charm hard, just like a streetwalker, and your friends all love you for it, but when it comes to the intimate reality of a sexual relationship, you just don't have anything to give. All you can do is take."

Larry's deflation was almost total. He sat on a chair and watched silently, like a sulking, spoiled child, as she packed. When she was ready to leave she stood before him and leaned over to kiss him chastely on his forehead.

"Goodbye, Larry."

"Goodbye, Orgy Girl," he said sadly.

The End

Just a few of our many titles for sale...

The Young Governess
The first title in our Past Venus Historical imprint. Kate Spencer's job as governess to a young girl in a large country house seemed idealic. However, she is soon drawn into the Followers – a mysterious group who take pleasure in forcing young women to perform perverse sexual rituals.
£7.50

Backdoor Virgins
After catching her husband with his flame-haired mistress, beautiful heiress Ellen Fielding is determined to seek revenge. Embarking on a nymphomatic spree of epic proportions, she not only loses her anal virginity but plans an erotic retribution for the two lovers that they will never forget.
£7.50

Nicole's Pregnant Hunger
On returning from her honeymoon, Nicole Ashby is delighted to learn she is pregnant. And pregnancy proves to be no obstacle to her insatiable lust either. But who could the father be? Not only is her husband in the running, but most of the men in his predatory family too.
£7.50

Salem's Daughters
The first title in our Past Venus Fantasy imprint. After centuries under the sod, warlock John Willard is more than ready to wreck vengeance on the decendants of the men and woman who sent him to the gallows, introducing them to incestuous perversions on a grand scale..
£7.50

Turkish Delight
After being cruelly raped by her callous husband on her honeymoon, Lucy Dean finds herself adrift in one of the most exciting and dangerous cities in the world: Istanbul. Drugged and abducted, she faces a life of sexual slavery, but first she must be taught the tricks of the trade.
£7.50

Orderline: 0800 026 25 24
Email: eps@leadline.co.uk
Post: EPS, 54 New Street, Worcester WR1 2DL

EPS

WWW.EROTICPRINTS.ORG